Guy Looked at Her with Anger . . . with Hunger.

He pulled her roughly onto the dance floor, and Aidan felt a clap of thunder in her heart that resonated through to her very soul. For an eternity their bodies swayed with the music, their eyes told secrets—so intimate, so close.

He bent to kiss her, and their lips clung as they stood together, scarcely moving in the amber-colored mist.

But before Aidan could say what was in her heart, the music ended and Guy let his arm drop.

Then he turned his back on her—and walked wordlessly away . . .

DOROTHY CORK
was born in Australia and has lived there most of her life. Her many readers may well have guessed this, as her entertaining novels are frequently set in her native land. Not that she limits herself to this region. She is an enthusiastic and perceptive traveler. Her wholehearted enjoyment of life is reflected in her lively romances.

Dear Reader:

Silhouette has always tried to give you exactly what you want. When you asked for increased realism, deeper characterization and greater length, we brought you Silhouette Special Editions. When you asked for increased sensuality, we brought you Silhouette Desire. Now you ask for books with the length and depth of Special Editions, the sensuality of Desire, but with something else besides, something that no one else offers. Now we bring you SILHOUETTE INTIMATE MOMENTS, true romance novels, longer than the usual, with all the depth that length requires. More sensuous than the usual, with characters whose maturity matches that sensuality. Books with the ingredient no one else has tapped: excitement.

There is an electricity between two people in love that makes everything they do magic, larger than life—and this is what we bring you in SILHOUETTE INTIMATE MOMENTS. Look for them this May, wherever you buy books.

These books are for the woman who wants more than she has ever had before. These books are for you. As always, we look forward to your comments and suggestions. You can write to me at the address below:

Karen Solem
Editor-in-Chief
Silhouette Books
P.O. Box 769
New York, N.Y. 10019

DOROTHY CORK
Island Spell

Silhouette Romance

Published by Silhouette Books New York

America's Publisher of Contemporary Romance

Other Silhouette Books by Dorothy Cork

Secret Marriage
By Honour Bound
Reluctant Deceiver
No More Regrets

 SILHOUETTE BOOKS, a Simon & Schuster Division of
GULF & WESTERN CORPORATION
1230 Avenue of the Americas, New York, N.Y. 10020

ISBN: 0-671-57219-9

First Silhouette Books printing April, 1983

10 9 8 7 6 5 4 3 2 1

Map by Ray Lundgren

America's Publisher of Contemporary Romance

Printed in the U.S.A.

Island
Spell

AUSTRALIA

Places set in _italics_ are fictitious.

Chapter One

Everyone except Aidan Elliot had moved along the jetty in the direction of the island resort, nestling in its tropical greenery beyond the white beach. Aidan watched them disappear, then leaned against the rail, trying to relax and glancing at her watch. She'd been told at the tourist agency at Mackay that she'd be picked up here on Wilcox Island at 4:30—presumably by Guy Desailley—which meant she had about ten minutes to stand there biting her nails and wondering how it was all going to turn out.

Lifting her head and thrusting back the soft brown hair that was blowing across her cheek, she saw that the Coral Queen was already moving off across the emerald and cobalt waters of the sea where other islands floated, brilliantly green under the tropic sun. Was one of those islands Breakaway, where she was to spend at least the next few weeks of her life? she wondered. She had no idea.

She had no idea either whether she was really likely to be just the secretary Guy Desailley wanted. Her cousin Shay had said she most certainly was, but somehow, now that she was so close to actually presenting herself, doubts had begun to grow in Aidan's mind.

With sudden nervousness, she dug into the zippered flight bag she'd balanced on top of her one large suitcase, and producing a small hand mirror, she looked at her reflection searchingly. Darkly lashed grey eyes looked back at her intently, and she curved her soft lips into a smile and then grimaced. It would be no use smiling at him. That would get her nowhere. It was performance at work that would count. Although surely she would satisfy him there.

Her mind slipped back to the telegram that had come from Breakaway Island only a couple of days ago, and which she knew by heart: *Please find me secretary urgently. You know type I want. Let me know arrival date. Will refund all travel and other expenses. Regards, Guy.*

Actually, the message was intended for Michael Hamilton, Shay's husband, but as he was visiting Perth on business and would be away for at least another week, Shay had decided she'd better deal with it. "Guy," she'd explained to Aidan, was the novelist Guy Desailley. She'd met him only once, though he'd been a friend of Michael's for years.

"You know, you could take this job, Aidan," she'd said brightly. "It's just what you've been looking for, isn't it?"

It was, of course, because until a month ago, when their aunt, Sylvia Barrett, had died after a long illness, through all of which she'd somehow gone on working, Aidan had been her secretary. Sylvia too had been a writer, though she wrote books for girls, whereas Guy Desailley wrote for a very different, very adult market.

Aidan had fairly recently read one of his novels, *Pressure,* after she'd seen the film made from it. She'd thought it terrific, but it hadn't appealed to the fastidious and slightly squeamish Sylvia. "Clever, but far too frank for my taste," Sylvia had commented after reading a couple of chapters, and had thankfully retreated to her own world.

"It sounds ideal," Aidan had agreed. "But do you really think I'm the type be wants? Don't you think we should wait till Michael comes back?" she'd queried, glancing again at the telegram.

They were in the Hamiltons' house, where she'd been staying since her aunt had died. She'd lived in Sylvia Barrett's home at Whale Beach for seven years, but now the house was to be sold and the proceeds from the sale given to an organisation that cared for crippled and disabled children. And although Michael and Shay were marvellous people to live with, at twenty-two Aidan still had to find work for herself as soon as she reasonably could.

"We can't possibly wait. It's urgent," Shay asserted. "But of course you're the right type. You'll suit Guy perfectly. You've had four years' experience in exactly the same kind of work. It would do you good to have a complete change and go up to North Queensland, anyhow. Get you away from Robert, too. He seems to upset you for some reason or other," she added a little uncomfortably, bending her blond head and studying her nails.

Robert Fuller did upset her. Aidan had been the one to suggest that they call off their engagement, but though he'd taken back the ring, he still continued to act as though he had the right to interfere in her life. He'd been furious when he discovered that Sylvia had left her not the house, not the continuing royalties from her books, but a mere five thousand dollars. The house, he'd asserted, was Aidan's by right, and when he'd insisted that she must contest the will, and she'd refused, he was so unpleasant about it that she had felt compelled to break off their engagement. Robert had protested in no more than a token manner, yet he still wouldn't let her alone, and was continually telephoning her or even calling at the Hamiltons' house and urging her to "do something" about what he called "that grossly unjust will that's robbed you of a lovely home." It began to seem to Aidan that he was far more concerned about losing the house than about losing her. And to be ruthlessly realistic, he hadn't asked her to marry him until it was discovered that Sylvia had a terminal illness.

It was all very disillusioning, but curiously, she wasn't brokenhearted at the thought of not marrying Robert, and she rather suspected that she'd never really been in love with him. She'd never told Shay exactly why the engagement was off, and how much the other girl knew or suspected she didn't know, but now she admitted, "It would be a good idea to go away. We should both start again, and somehow it seems impossible the way things are. We're not going to patch it up. I'm quite sure of that. I know Aunt Sylvia was convinced we'd marry and live happily ever after, but it just hasn't worked out like that." She looked at Shay wryly and shrugged her slim shoulders.

"It's plain why she left the house to charity instead of to you, of course," Shay said. "She thought you'd be well provided for, since Robert's family's so well off and he's the only child. I'm really sorry it's happened like this, Aidan. It doesn't seem fair, considering that you'd lived with Aunt all those years and worked for her ever since you left school."

"Don't talk like that," Aidan said sharply. "Sylvia

left me five thousand dollars, remember. She was wonderful to work for and she taught me a lot. She paid me well, and she was always making me lavish gifts of clothing and jewelry and so on. I have no complaints at all about how I've been treated. Anyhow let's get back to this job and Guy Desailley, because I *am* interested. What's he like? You said you've met him . . ."

"Only once—in Spain two years ago when Mike and I were on our honeymoon. He's dishy—really dishy—in a terribly masculine sort of way. He's been married once, but his wife was killed in a car accident, I think. That's why he went overseas—to get over it. He's been dividing his time between England and Spain for about four years, but Mike says he's decided to settle down in Australia again. I gather he wants to buy a house in Sydney when he's had enough of Breakaway Island. Anyhow, you'll like him, Aidan, I'm sure. And think of working on a tropical island! Shall I send him a telegram right away and tell him you're coming?"

"Not till it's all fixed up," Aidan protested laughing. "I must admit it all sounds too good to miss. And even if it doesn't work out to be permanent, at least it will be a new experience."

So now, just two days later, here she was waiting for the dishy Guy Desailley to come and pick her up and take her to Breakaway Island.

Robert had stopped in at the Hamiltons' home the night before, and Shay had left him to talk to Aidan privately. He was an architect working with his father's firm and was already making a name for himself through his original and creative work. He'd more than once talked enthusiastically to Aidan of what could be done with her aunt's house at Whale Beach. It had a spectacular view over the Pacific Ocean, and could be made into a magnificent showplace—if enough money were spent on it. That would have been possible if Robert had acquired the property through Aidan. As it was, she knew that Mr. Fuller was not prepared to pay the price that was being asked for it.

Aidan had left her packing and listened while he invited her to come out to dinner with him at Jonah's restaurant.

"I've booked a table for two. I couldn't get you on the phone, but I thought you might feel like an outing."

"Sorry, Robert. I can't come. I have some packing to do. You see, I'm going away tomorrow."

"Going away? Where to?" he wanted to know. He was tall, thinnish, with a clever, good-looking face that had a touch of conceit about it.

"I'm going to North Queensland," Aidan said. "I've landed a job on one of the islands off the Whitsunday Coast."

"Good heavens! Why on earth do you want to go there?" he exclaimed, frowning. "You don't know anyone there, do you?"

"Not a soul—as yet," she admitted. "But I thought it sounded exciting, and after all, I'm perfectly free to come and go as I choose these days, aren't I?"

"You mean since our engagement's off? Well, that was your idea, not mine," he said, and Aidan sighed inwardly. He sounded so accusing, yet she knew his heart was far from broken. "So what are you going to do on this island, anyhow?"

"More or less what I did for Aunt Sylvia. I'm going to be secretary to a novelist. To Guy Desailley, as a matter of fact."

He stared at her as if she'd said she was going to Mars.

"Guy Desailley! How ever did you get mixed up with him? What was that movie we saw . . . ?"

"Pressure," she said.

"Pressure," he repeated slowly. "I can't imagine *you* working for a man who writes that kind of thing, Aidan."

Aidan shrugged. "Don't worry. I have a personal recommendation. He's an old friend of Michael's. Shay's met him and she says he's very nice, so I'm prepared to see how it works out. It mightn't be permanent, of course, and he's only living on this island temporarily. He means to settle in Sydney eventually, I believe."

Robert's eyes narrowed. "You're determined to break with me, aren't you? Yet all I want is to see that you're not cheated."

"I have broken with you, Robert," she said, raising her eyebrows. "And I don't feel I've been cheated. I'm perfectly happy about my Aunt's will. I need a job, that's all, and this one sounds interesting."

There was a pause, pregnant with Robert's disapproval, and finally Aidan said stiffly, "You'd better go now, or your table won't be kept for you."

"That hardly matters, does it, since you aren't coming out with me," he said curtly, but he got to his feet. "Leave me your address, will you? I might drop you a line."

She bit her lip. "I'd rather you didn't do that, Robert. I'd far sooner you forgot about me and left me to manage my own life."

He laughed briefly. "Quite obviously you don't have a clue how to do that, Aidan. I seem to be the only one who cares a cent about looking after your interests. However, if that's the way you want it, there's nothing I can do . . ."

Aidan leaned against the rail of the jetty and stared out over the jewelled sea. She hoped fervently that

Robert wouldn't bother her anymore. It would be far better if he forgot all about her and the house at Whale Beach and found himself another girl and another interest. At any rate, she wasn't going to waste any more of her time thinking about him, that was for sure.

She straightened suddenly, feeling her pulses quicken. A small launch was heading toward the jetty! It must be Guy Desailley, and in a few short minutes she'd know what she was letting herself in for. She'd have to be on her toes and demonstrate to her employer that she was just the kind of secretary he wanted. She had a sneaking suspicion that matchmaking had been lurking somewhere at the back of Shay's mind, but she certainly wasn't in a hurry to get herself involved with a man again. First and foremost she was here to work, to gain more experience, and she was determined to be the ultimate in efficiency. Not for a moment was she going to trade on the fact that her cousin was married to a close friend of her new boss.

When the launch came up to the jetty, she saw that there was only one person aboard. A man with a dark beard. He looked about fifty, and unexpectedly her heart plummetted. She'd imagined him to be about the same age as Michael, somewhere in the early or middle thirties, and she was disappointed. If this was Guy Desailley, then Shay had a strange idea of dishiness. But perhaps he hadn't worn that beard two years ago. Anyhow, she thought, rather annoyed with herself, did it really matter what he looked like? She was here to work for him, not to fall in love with him, and that was the way she wanted it to be.

He sprang onto the jetty in an agile way, and she told herself he looked nice. Not like a writer, but then after all, a writer was only a human being. Sylvia hadn't looked like a writer either. He wore a white T-shirt and white shorts, and his legs, like his arms, were brown and hairy and muscular. His eyes were blue and rather screwed up.

"Miss Elliot?" He halted a few paces from her. His voice was typically Australian, and he looked at her hard and smiled briefly as she admitted a shade reluctantly, "Yes, that's right. You must be Mr. Desailley."

"Afraid not. I'm Brian Hardy, from the Breakaway Resort."

"Oh." Aidan actually wanted to laugh. She expelled her breath gently and sent him a bright smile. "I took it for granted Mr. Desailley would be meeting me."

"I guess you did. But Guy's not around today. He's apt to go walkabout now and again without telling anyone. I took the telegram saying you were arriving over the phone this morning. It arrived too late last night—our telephone communications with the mainland close down at six."

His smile enveloped her briefly; his eyes skimmed over her slight figure in the pale-tan crinkle-cotton dress, taking in her beige bag and matching sandals, and somehow she knew he was aware she was well and expensively dressed. That was thanks to Sylvia, for her aunt had been interested in fashion, and it had pleased her to see her niece well dressed.

"I hadn't expected anyone so young," Brian Hardy commented as he picked up her two pieces of luggage. "Go ahead, will you? Hop on board and sit down."

Aidan did as he said. She was quite ridiculously pleased to find he wasn't Guy Desailley after all, though it was probably because Shay's description of Guy had raised her expectations. But quite decidedly she wasn't looking for romance. This was strictly business. On a tropical island resort, she thought, wryly amused at herself.

In a couple of minutes they were off across the water, Aidan's hair flying about her head as she looked around with eager interest.

"I suppose you're wondering where I fit into the picture," Brian Hardy called back to her presently. She wasn't; in fact, she hadn't been thinking about him at all, but she didn't enlighten him. "I run the resort on Breakaway Island. My wife and I lease it from Guy Desailley—have done for a few years now. You probably know he owns the island. It belonged to his family before him."

"I didn't know that," Aidan called back, interested after all. It was something that Shay hadn't told her and probably hadn't known. "Have we far to go?"

"Another twenty mintues or so. Breakaway's one of a small group well out toward the Great Barrier Reef, but not all that near it. Have you been up here before?"

"Never. I haven't been north of Brisbane. I'm from Sydney."

"You don't know Guy Desailley?" He'd turned his head round to give her a long, hard look from his bright-blue eyes.

Aidan shook her head, leaning back in the seat. "All I know is that he needs a secretary. Was there—was there someone there before?"

"Yeah. An Englishwoman." He said it with a shrug. He had beefy, brawny shoulders, leathery skin, and blue eyes surrounded by wrinkles. His hair was cut short and was still untouched by grey, and there was dark hair on the backs of his hands. "She left a few days ago. Went back to England." He turned his back and offered no more information.

A few minutes later, after they'd passed several large islands, all of them looking completely uninhabited, he pointed ahead.

"That's Breakaway. The largest of the three islands."

Aidan narrowed her eyes and saw vague shapes floating on the transparent sheet of sea, softly blurred indigo silhouettes against a background of dark clouds that were banking up low on the horizon. How remote and unreal it all looked, and how strange it seemed that she should be heading out into the blue distance this way, leaving behind her everyone and everything she knew. She hoped that she'd hit it off with her new employer. Working together would be impossible if she didn't. She remembered a secretary Sylvia had once had, while Aidan was still at school. An ordinary and likable enough woman, and yet Sylvia couldn't stand her. It had been as if a shark had been put in a platypus's pool. She'd stayed a week, and that was it.

Well, *she* wasn't coming all this way and staying only a week. She'd just make a point of getting on with Guy Desailley, that was all. But it looked like such a tiny island; they'd be so cut off from the world.

"Do many people come to the resort, Mr. Hardy?" she asked a little nervously.

"Sure they do. As many as we can accommodate almost all year. It's not as small as you're probably imagining. We have a very good setup; everything's modern, and fortunately there's plenty of water on the island. It's a popular place with fishermen and anyone who wants to get right away from everything—people with plenty of money who need a break from the pressures of civilisation. I wouldn't live anywhere else myself, though it's not everyone's cup of tea as a permanent residence. You either love it or you hate it."

I'll love it, Aidan thought determinedly. At least until Guy Desailley decides to go down to Sydney.

It was a beautiful little island, she thought as they

17

came nearer to it. Scalloped beaches adorned its shores, and the dazzling white sand was softened to a pearly colour by the late-afternoon light. Tropical greenery covered an unexpectedly high hill, though not really unexpectedly, since it was a continental island whose heights had once overlooked valleys that were now drowned by the reef-sheltered sea. The launch glided over waters as pale and clear a green as chryso-prase, and breathtakingly lovely. Leaning over the side of the boat, Aidan could see the darkness of the fringing coral reef deep down, and brilliantly coloured fish, some of them quite large. Soon on the island she could discern people under the coconut palms and dwellings half hidden in the shadows, but instead of taking the launch toward the small jetty, Brian Hardy was heading it along by the shore in the direction of a small rocky headland.

"That's the Breakaway Resort, Miss Elliot, but I'm taking you round to Desailley's beach. Guy may be back by now, with a bit of luck."

Aidan felt a tremor of nervousness. It hadn't oc-curred to her before that Guy mightn't be living at the resort.

Once they'd rounded the rocky promontory, another beach came into view, pandanus palms and casuarinas crowding thickly along it. The jetty here looked some-what more fragile than the one at the resort, and a large notice announced, Private Property. No Landing Here.

"Can't be back yet," Brian muttered. "The boat's not here. What do you think, Miss Elliot? Shall I take you back to the resort, or do you want to wait?"

Aidan made up her mind quickly. "I think I'd better wait. He's expecting me." Expecting *someone,* she amended mentally. "He's sure to be back soon, isn't he?"

"I couldn't say. But as you please." He manoeuvred the boat expertly, brought it in alongside the jetty, secured it and came to get her luggage. "What do you want me to do about this?"

Aidan had no idea. She wished Guy Desailley were here to take charge. She shaded her eyes with her hand and looked across the sparkling sand. She could see a large bungalow built of stained timber merging gracefully into the background of what looked like a tropical garden grown wild. Guy Desailley's bungalow, presumably. She was hardly going to settle herself and all her possessions there, so she said decisively, "You can take my big suitcase back with you, if you would. If Mr. Desailley doesn't turn up, is there some way I can contact you and have someone come and fetch me?"

"Sure. There's a telephone through to the lodge. If you need me, just give me a ring and I'll come round and fetch you. Do you want me to come across to the bungalow with you?"

"Oh, no, please don't bother." She picked up her flight bag, deciding she'd take that with her at any rate, and Brian gave her a hand and helped her onto the jetty.

"Better not wander too far from the bungalow," was his parting advice. "It looks like there's a storm brewing. We get plenty of those in the late afternoons at this time of year, and you won't want to be drenched." He raised his hand in a farewell salute. "I'll be seeing you, Miss Elliot."

The launch moved off; Aidan made her way to the end of the jetty and a moment later was trudging through the sand. Its heat burned through the thin soles of her sandals, and the sun blazed down on her uncovered head. She could feel the storm in the air and blamed her edginess on that. And too, she was quite exhausted. She'd had a hectic two days, and she'd travelled over 2,000 kilometres since she'd left home this morning. "It's urgent," Shay had insisted. And now he wasn't even here. Everything had been arranged in such a mad rush, and Aidan herself had sent the telegram yesterday afternoon, signing it Hamilton on Shay's advice. "He doesn't have to know it wasn't Michael who arranged for you to come," she'd said.

Aidan reached the shade of the palms and followed the path to the bungalow. She climbed the steps onto a shady verandah with a tiled floor and collapsed into a cane chair. What a welcome! No one here.

After a few moments she got up and discovered, not surprisingly, that the door was wide open. After all, who'd lock up in a place like this? She pushed open the screen door and called out, but there was no answer. Inside, the hallway smelt of the sea, and there was sand on the floor. The first door led into a big sitting room that had wide windows looking across the verandah to the beach. The view was picturesque but lacked the dramatic quality that its height above the sea gave to the house where she'd lived with her aunt. There were books everywhere and original paintings on the walls— watercolours that appeared to have been done on or around the island.

This house and its furnishings have been here for a long time, she thought. The furniture was old but good, most of it cedar, and most of it obviously handmade. New curtains and new covers for the chairs were plainly needed, but the room was attractive just the same. It was very hot and humid, and she glanced up at the big ceiling fan but didn't turn it on. What she really needed, she decided, was a long, cold drink.

She located the kitchen, big and comfortable-looking with a modern stove, a freezer and a fridge. And a stack of unwashed dishes on the draining board beside the sink. In the fridge she found a big covered jug of pineapple juice.

Fresh mangoes in a bowl on the table scented the air deliciously as she poured herself a glass of juice. She drank half of it thirstily and then wandered through the house, looking into every room.

At the door of the room that was obviously Guy Desailley's bedroom she paused curiously, as if hoping to get some inkling as to what kind of man he was. On the whole, it wasn't an aggressively masculine room. There were blue rugs on the polished floor, blue and white striped curtains and a dark-blue quilt on the double bed. A pair of crumpled jeans was slung over the back of a cane armchair; there was a book on the floor by the bed and a notebook on the bedside table. Brushes and combs and a couple of toiletries—plus a small pile of books—graced the dressing table, and a group of framed photographs decorated one wall. But even from the doorway, Aidan could see that the photographs were old and had most likely belonged to his family. There was not one that looked as if it could be a portrait of his wife.

Feeling suddenly as if she were prying, she moved on quickly.

The next room was a bathroom, and beyond that was a large room instantly recognisable as Guy's study. On the desk was a pile of manuscript pages, a thick scribble pad and a rather beat-up typewriter. There was no second desk for a secretary, as there had been in Sylvia's study, so apparently the secretary must have a room of her own.

It was on the other side of the hall, much smaller but well equipped, with a more modern-looking electric typewriter and large table that served as a desk. French doors led onto the side verandah, and another door opened into a bedroom that had its own bathroom. It was a charming room, decorated in pale gold and a soft, muted green that set off the light furniture, and there was an unusual heart-shaped mirror with a gilt frame over the dressing table. As with the adjoining office, French windows looked across the verandah through a shady side garden to the beach, away from the jetty. The sun had gone, and quite definitely a storm was coming up. Brian had been right.

Aidan had scarcely gone back through the house to the front verandah when there was a crash of thunder and the rain began to fall in torrents. In minutes the dirt paths in the garden were running with water, and the air was full of the scent of frangipani flowers and steaming earth. Aidan stood for some time listening to the drumming of the rain on the roof, watching the leaves of the banana plants sway and bow as the water ran down them in rivulets, watching the bright red-gold flowers of the poinciana trees fall to the ground, bruised and broken.

The deluge hadn't abated when at last she went inside for another drink. She wondered if she should telephone Brian Hardy. She had a feeling that Guy Desailley was never going to materialise, that she'd wasted her time coming all this way. The air inside the house was steamy, but she didn't turn on the ceiling fan in the kitchen. It was hardly worthwhile now, she thought, feeling more than a little depressed and let down.

As she drank her fruit juice thirstily, she suddenly stiffened. Through the sound of the rain she could hear someone in the house, and her heart began to pound. It must be Guy Desailley. She set her glass down on the sink with a hand that trembled slightly, ran her fingers through her hair and moistened her lips nervously. He'd be surprised to find her here. Her flight bag was in the kitchen, and there was no sign that anyone was there. She hadn't even switched on a light.

She reached the door of the sitting room to discover a man standing there. His torso was bare and he was in the act of pulling down the zipper of the sodden jeans that clung tightly to his muscular thighs. He looked at her across the room.

She stood stock still. So this was Guy Desailley. Nothing Shay had said had prepared her for such shatteringly good looks. His face was tanned and hard, his hair black and thick and curly and at this moment dripping with water. He had a wide mouth, its hardness relieved by a sensually full lower lip; his jaw was firm and aggressive, and he badly needed a shave.

The eyes that met and held hers compellingly were so dark, they were almost black. Black and penetrating and inscrutable. And also vaguely angry.

No, not vaguely angry, she suddenly realised. Very definitely angry. Aidan was sure that if she'd brought that glass of fruit juice with her, she'd have dropped it. The air was electric and it wasn't the storm. Her ears hummed as the blood pounded through her veins.

Slowly he drew up the zipper of his pants and came across the room toward her on his bare feet.

"Who the hell are you and what are you doing in my bungalow?"

Aidan swallowed and discovered that she was temporarily incapable of speech.

"Well?" His eyes moved over her inimically, and from as close as this, she saw that they were not black, but a dark, inky blue. "If you're from the resort, then run along back there. You're trespassing and you know it. You can read. Now get moving. Go back the way you came and don't tell me it's raining. I don't care if you get wet."

Aidan felt the colour rise slowly to her cheeks. So he

thought she was a tourist from the resort invading his privacy. She was thankful she wasn't. As it was, she felt like sinking through the floor, and her first impression of him had already taken a definite knock. He was evidently a man of action as well as a writer! He didn't stop to think she might have some good reason for being here. Attack first, find out later, she thought, and told him dryly, "I'm not from the resort, Mr. Desailley. I'm Aidan Elliot, and I'm sorry I walked in on you like that just now."

His eyebrows rose satanically. "Another moment and you'd have been even sorrier. I'd have been stark naked. . . . So who are you? Should your name mean something to me? I hope you're not a budding journalist, because I'm not available for interviews."

She bit her lip. "I'm not a journalist. If you'd been here this morning, you'd have known my name from Michael Hamilton's telegram. I've come to work for you."

"What?" he exclaimed sharply. The storm had made the room half dark and he strode across and switched on the light and the ceiling fan; then he turned back to look at her, taking her in thoroughly, his mouth twisting cynically. His eyes travelled down her slender form and then returned to her flushed cheeks, her grey eyes framed by dark lashes.

"Michael sent *you* to work for me? I don't believe it."

Aidan's flush deepened. Michael hadn't sent her, of course, though he would have if he'd been around. She had excellent qualifications, and Shay had been quite positive she was just the sort of girl Guy Desailley was looking for.

"Why shouldn't you believe it?" she demanded, her head up.

"I'll tell you why not," he said. He put his hands on his narrow hips and his dark eyes glittered as he looked at her. "Because Michael would know damned well you're just the kind of girl I'm *not* interested in. A pretty girl fresh from secretarial college with a head full of romance and not a clue as to what this kind of position entails. I can tell by looking at you—and by the way you've been looking at me—that you'll be of no use to me. What did you say your name was?"

"Aidan Elliot," she said, beginning to feel angry.

"So how did you persuade Michael to send you along to work for me, Aidan Elliot? And why?" he asked, leaning his broad shoulders against the wall.

"I didn't persuade him," she said quite truthfully. "The job came up, it was offered to me and I accepted it. I assure you I'm not just out of secretarial school, Mr. Desailley. I'm fully qualified to work for you."

"Are you indeed?" One eyebrow rose quizzically. "Well, before we go into that in depth, I'm going to get into some dry clothes. While I do that you can demonstrate your specialised qualifications by pouring me a drink. Whisky. Take it out to the verandah. Get something for yourself too. You're beginning to look as if you need it. I'll join you in a few minutes."

He disappeared and Aidan looked round the room quickly. There was a cabinet that looked as if it might hold drinks—and did. She found the whisky bottle and a glass and then went into the kitchen. She put water into a small jug, some ice cubes in a pitcher, and collected a tray and the fruit drink she'd already poured for herself, topping it up. She didn't need any alcohol. She preferred to keep her brain clear while she was sorting out the situation with this difficult man. She wasn't going to impress him if she couldn't think straight.

On the verandah, she deposited the tray on a cane table and waited for him, looking out at the sea that had been so brilliantly coloured when she'd arrived and now was scarcely visible. All she could see was a grey blur with the dark shapes of the palms slashed across it, their long fronds moving wildly under the onslaught of the storm. The sound of the rain drummed out every other sound. The air was hot and humid, and she felt perspiration on her upper lip and in the crook of her elbows.

"Well, pour it out." Guy Desailley had joined her, and she started slightly. For a moment she didn't know if he were talking about his drink or her story. His drink, of course, she realised, pulling herself together and moving quickly to do as he said. Obviously he wasn't going to tell her how he liked his whisky. One of the qualifications for a position with him was evidently that you must be a mind reader. She wasn't going to be too hasty and take it for granted he liked his whisky on the rocks. Sylvia's publisher had been a whisky drinker, and he liked his whisky neat. For all she knew, Guy Desailley might have the same taste, so she poured a measure of the spirit into the glass and handed it to him wordlessly, leaving him to add water or ice as he chose.

She'd done right. He took neither, and as he took the glass he looked at her across it, his glance intent and curious, and very disconcerting. He'd changed into tight-fitting white jeans, but he was still barefoot and bare-chested, a gold chain glinting against the dark mat of hair on his chest. He hadn't shaved, and the darkness of his jaw gave him a tough look.

How on earth am I going to cope with a man like this? Aidan wondered with a slight shiver of apprehension. She thought of the house at Whale Beach where she'd lived for seven years, of her small, slim, delicate aunt, with her elegant slightly passé look and her innocent mind, and she was suddenly aware that working for Guy Desailley was going to be a completely different proposition.

"Sit down," he told her, and she sat. He took a chair too, to her relief. It would have been just too much to have him stand staring down at her. He stretched his long legs out in front of him, swallowed down his whisky and then looked at her with deceptive laziness.

"Right," he said. "Now let's hear the full story. To begin with, I want to know how Michael came to send you up here."

She widened her eyes. "I've already told you. You asked him to find you a secretary."

"And practically by return mail—before I've had time to turn round and blink—you're here."

"You should be pleased," she exclaimed. "You said it was urgent, and since I had the experience, and happened to be free, and needed the work, Mr. Hamilton asked me to take it on."

"Again—I don't believe you," he said flatly.

Aidan flushed deeply. The trouble was, it wasn't altogether true, yet why should it matter that it hadn't actually been Michael who'd chosen her? She set down her glass on the table, with a hand that shook.

"So now let's hear the truth," he said and waited.

Aidan sighed and gave in to the inevitable. "Well, Mr. Hamilton's in Perth on business just now," she admitted uneasily. "Shay—his wife—is looking after things for him, and it was she who arranged for me to take this position."

Guy Desailley smiled crookedly, his teeth white against the tan of his skin.

"And of course you leaped at it." He got up from his chair to pour himself another whisky. The storm was easing off; steam was beginning to rise from the ground; the big-leafed trees dripped water. Aidan swallowed some more of her fruit juice.

"You mentioned qualifications, Miss Elliot." He hadn't sat down again but stood looking down at her intently. "What are they? Apart from the fact that you're an extremely pretty girl," he added, his eyes trailing over her deliberately.

Aidan counted ten.

"I do have qualifications, Mr. Desailley. I've been secretary to a writer—a novelist—for the past four years."

"You must have started young." His glance tilted over her small, firm breasts, her long, lightly tanned legs; she stiffened slightly.

"I was eighteen."

"Which makes you still very young. . . . You have references, of course?"

She bit her lip. "No. My employer died just recently. She was Sylvia Barrett," she added.

His eyebrows rose. "Who the hell is she?"

Aidan sighed. "You may not have heard of her, but I assure you she's very well known. She writes—wrote—books for girls." She'd almost said "young adults," but it was a phrase Sylvia had never used. "I write for *girls,*" she'd always insisted firmly. "The normal girls who still exist, whatever books like *Puberty Blues* may lead you to believe."

"And you feel that typing out stories for kids, written by some nice little old lady, fits you to work for me, do you? And Shay Hamilton thinks so too. Well, I've met Shay only once, but I must admit she struck me as being something of a dumb blonde. I conclude I was right."

"You were not right," Aidan exclaimed indignantly. "Shay's——"

"You know her personally, do you?" he interrupted, leaning back on the verandah rail.

"Yes, I do," she snapped, and hurried on without thinking. "As it happens, she's my cousin."

His long mouth twisted up at one corner. "Really? Well, well! It happens very neatly, doesn't it? In fact, I'm beginning to get a very clear picture of the whole thing. It would seem that you and your cousin got together and decided . . ."

"We didn't get together and decide anything," Aidan said heatedly. "I've just told you—or tried to tell you—that my working background qualifies me for this position. I've read only a couple of your books, but I really can't see why working for you should be a great deal different from working for Sylvia Barrett," she finished flatly and was amazed at her own temerity in asserting so firmly something that by now she didn't believe at all.

He looked at her quizzically. "Can't you, Miss Elliot? You may very well find that what I want and what Miss Barrett wanted are two completely different things."

"Really? Then what is your taste in secretaries?" she demanded.

"My taste?" His nostrils flared. "I don't have a taste in secretaries. We're not talking about bedmates, you know. We're talking about someone who's going to have to work for—and with—me."

"Then why shouldn't I qualify?"

He narrowed his eyes and regarded her coldly. "For a number of reasons, which Michael would know."

"Is that all you can say?" she exclaimed scornfully.

"I don't have to say a thing," he told her.

Aidan sprang to her feet. "You're impossible! Well, I can tell you this—I wouldn't want to work for you if it were my last chance at finding a job . . . and right now

I'd like to use your telephone. I'm leaving. I didn't come all this way to work for a male chauvinist." She rushed toward the door, but before she reached it, he'd grabbed her from behind, his arms locked around her waist.

"Just simmer down, will you, Miss Elliot?" he said softly.

She could feel the warmth of his breath on the top of her head, and she tried ineffectually to wrench herself away from him. "I won't simmer down," she said through her teeth. "Let go of me at once."

"I'll let go of you when you're ready to sit down and talk like a rational human being," he gritted.

"*I'm* ready, but *you* aren't," she panted. Then she added illogically, "Besides, there's nothing to talk about. Obviously, I've wasted my time coming here." She was acutely conscious of his fingers on her hip-bones, of the warmth of his body pressed against the length of her back, of the fact that his closeness was making it impossible for her to think at all. With a sudden violent movement she broke away from him to stand trembling as he moved to block the doorway. "Let me pass. It's getting dark. I want to get away from here."

"If you're thinking of running off to the lodge—of leaving tomorrow—you can think again, Miss Elliot," he said, his voice hard. "The cost of bringing you here is mine, and I'm the one who'll decide whether you stay or not."

"I thought you had decided." Her breathing quickened as his dark-blue eyes journeyed to her vulnerable mouth and rested there. She knew he was going to kiss her. Men had looked at her that way before. She wasn't entirely unsophisticated. She tensed as he raised his eyes slowly until they met hers. That sexy look she'd been expecting was there, and she drew a sharp breath.

She knew that in spite of everything she found him attractive, physically at least, and she was far from unresponsive to him. It was a purely mechanical thing, something that couldn't be helped but could be understood and then disregarded. So he needn't think she'd fall into his arms if he reached for her. Her lips had parted, and with a slight shock she realised he probably knew the sort of thing that was going on in her mind, and she looked away hastily.

To her chagrin, since she was braced to resist him, he made no move to touch her. Instead, he said something that took her completely by surprise.

Chapter Two

"I'm going to give you a trial, Miss Elliot. I shall be interested in seeing how well you live up to your own opinion of yourself."

His voice was cool and his words struck her like a dash of cold water. She stared at him in disbelief, sure that she must be hearing things. She hadn't imagined for a single moment that he'd be fair enough to give her a chance to prove herself, and now she was torn by indecision. On one hand, she wanted to walk out on him, to leave him stranded, to show him he couldn't treat her this way and get away with it. But on the other hand, it would give her a great deal of satisfaction to prove that she was very efficient at her work and that Shay was not the dumb blonde he seemed to think her. In fact, she'd like to make him eat his words.

As well, there was some incomprehensible factor working away at the back of her mind, telling her to stay—to stay.

"I'll think about it," she said finally.

He smiled mockingly. "I understood you did all your thinking a couple of days ago, Miss Elliot. It's a little late now to change your mind. You accepted this position when you came here, though it rests with me how long you stay. I wonder how much you found out about me before you packed your bags? Did your cousin give you a résumé of my reputation in general, of my . . . matrimonial status? Of my romantic history? Those are the things that interest women, aren't they?"

Aidan swallowed, vaguely aware that he was trying to pin something on her. The sort of thing that would probably be confirmed if he knew that Shay had told her he was dishy.

"I'm not interested in your personal life," she said stiffly.

"Perhaps you should be," he said mockingly, "since we're going to be so closely associated."

"I shall only be working for you," she said uneasily. "And now, do I have your permission to use the telephone and ring Mr. Hardy? My luggage is at the resort, and I can't stay here all night."

An expression of amusement crossed his face. "Staying here in this bungalow is part of the deal, Miss Elliot. My secretaries always live in—as Michael very well knows. And if you're afraid I might try to make love to you, that sort of thing doesn't have to be kept till after dark and bedtime. It can happen at any hour of the day. However, I want a secretary, not a mistress. I don't know what your responsibilities were with Miss Barrett, whether you lived in or not, or whether you had set hours of work. Here, you'll be on call more or less twenty-four hours a day—typing, correcting my blunders, preparing my meals. Doing anything and everything I might require of you, in fact. Sharing my recreation with me on the odd occasion, keeping intruders away. Do you really imagine you could handle all that if you slept over at the resort? Or was that part of the attraction in coming here? Did you see it all as a kind of glorious paid holiday?"

"Don't be ridiculous," Aidan exclaimed. "Of course I didn't. I . . . I didn't know what the island was like; I still don't. It might have been almost deserted as far as I knew."

"Then it was solely on my account you came?" he said with a smile that was maddening. And before she could think of a suitable retort, he asked unexpectedly, "Can you cook?"

She blinked in surprise. "Yes."

"Good. The art of cooking doesn't rate high among my talents. You can go out to the kitchen now and get me a meal. I haven't eaten all day and I'm hungry. Do you know which room is my study?"

Aidan hesitated. But he probably realised she'd had a good look around the bungalow before he came back. "Yes," she admitted.

"Bring it to me there," he said.

He strode past her and she stood staring after him. He wanted her to start work already. And remembering the clutter in the kitchen, she supposed it must be her responsibility to clear it up. Well, that didn't worry her in the least. He'd soon discover he had little to complain about regarding her efficiency and her willingness to do anything and everything, just as she had for Sylvia. She discovered she no longer wanted to walk out on him. The challenge of staying and proving him wrong appealed to her strongly. And remembering the way he'd looked at her not many minutes ago, she knew too that there was something else that held her here—perhaps the spice of danger she sensed in working for such a man, in living alone in the bungalow with him.

In the kitchen she found vegetables and some succulent-looking steak, and once she'd got the dinner under way she washed the pile of used dishes that had accumulated. She wondered how he liked his steak cooked, but knew better than to go and ask him. If she knew anything about writers, he wouldn't thank her for interrupting him. Her aunt, too, even when she was ill, had had a habit of disappearing into her study at odd hours, often just at dinnertime. She was used to it.

So Mr. Guy Desailley would have to tolerate his steak just the way she cooked it for him, she decided, and that would be medium rare. After tonight, it would be up to him to let her know if he had any special likes and dislikes.

She was just about to start cooking the steak when the telephone rang, and she listened to it uncertainly.

"Answer that telephone," Guy shouted irritably, and she grimaced.

"I'm on my way," she called back, but she didn't run.

It was Brian Hardy.

"Is that you, Miss Elliot? How are you getting on over there? Did Guy come back?"

"Oh, er . . . yes. I should have let you know. I . . . I won't bother about my luggage tonight, Mr. Hardy. Mr. Desailley's working and I have all I want for overnight. There's nothing really important in my suitcase." Only my pyjamas, she thought, my robe, my clean underthings, something to change into tomorrow.

There was a brief silence. "You mean you're going to stay at the bungalow?"

"Of course," she said crisply. "Didn't the last secretary stay here?"

"She did. But Diane was considerably older than you and a whole lot more sophisticated. However, it's up to you. . . . What do you want me to do about your luggage? Bring it over in the morning?"

"I'll let you know," Aidan said, deciding that it was something she'd have to consult her employer about. Just possibly, he mightn't want even Brian Hardy intruding on his privacy! On the other hand, he mightn't care to spare the time to fetch her luggage himself, or even to allow her to take the boat around for it. She had done some boating on Pitt Water and was quite capable of handling a small boat with an outboard motor, though of course Guy Desailley's boat might not be as simple as that.

"Thanks for calling, anyhow," she concluded. "Everything's just fine over here."

"I'm pleased to hear it," he said a little coldly. "Good night."

"Good night." She hung up and took a deep breath. *He* didn't think it was the thing for her to stay here alone with Guy Desailley. That was obvious. But Diane had done just that, and she couldn't see that it made much difference that Diane was older. Considerably older. What did *that* mean? That she was middle-aged? No longer attractive? Somehow she couldn't imagine such a woman being employed by Guy Desailley, and as she went back to the kitchen she wondered exactly why her predecessor had left.

When Aidan took his meal in to him a little later on, Guy took no notice of her at all. She left the tray on a side table and went out quietly, leaving the door half open, as it had been when she'd come in.

She ate her own meal in an annex near the kitchen, a sort of breakfast room. It was really part of the verandah, protected from the night by nothing but insect screening, and the light that she switched on illuminated part of the wild tropical garden eerily. Otherwise it was pitch-dark outside, the sky cloudy and starless, and there was the sound of water dripping everywhere, but the perfumes of flowers and fruits permeated the room delectably. She wondered idly how far away the resort was. It couldn't be all that far, though too far to walk carrying her heavy suitcase. Sometime, when she'd settled in, she'd definitely wander round there. It would be a break from work, a break from Guy Desailley.

When she took his coffee in to him, he'd eaten his meal, but he didn't compliment her or even thank her, and after a second she picked up the tray and went out.

Later, with her kitchen chores completed, she went onto the front verandah. Guy was still in his study and for that she was thankful. Through the dripping of water, Aidan could hear frogs croaking and the soft sound of the waves breaking on the shore. The beach gleamed silver through the palms, and far off across the water a distant light flickered like a small star. She thought about taking a walk but decided against it. She still had to arrange her sleeping accommodation, for obviously she was not going to be given any instructions about that. She'd use the bedroom attached to the small study, of course, but she'd have to find her own bed linen and so on.

The bed, she presently discovered, was already made up with fresh, sweet-smelling sheets, and she realised how exhausted she was. She'd left Sydney only that morning, yet everything familiar seemed to have receded so far, it was incredible.

Tomorrow, she reflected as, having stripped off her clothes, she stepped under the shower, her trial period would really begin. And tired as she was, she could hardly wait to prove to Guy Desailley that as a secretary, she'd leave nothing to be desired.

* * *

She slept deeply and dreamlessly; then, just before she woke she dreamed that someone took hold of her hands and drew her into a dance—a mad, dangerous dance, though exactly why it was dangerous she didn't know. Other girls, skirts flaring, hair floating, whirled by with invisible partners. Her partner was the only one with a face and his face was . . .

She opened her eyes and stared. The man she'd been dancing with stood looking down at her. His dark, curling hair fell across his forehead softly as if he hadn't combed it since he woke, and his chest above a pair of blue jeans was bare and muscular. She started to sit up and then retreated in confusion as she remembered she'd discarded her slip almost the minute she got into bed, it had been so hot and humid. Now the ceiling fan was whirring and she realised that Guy must have turned it on and that it probably had something to do with her dream.

"What . . . what do you want?" she asked stupidly, and then everything that had happened the day before came back into her mind as clearly as though it had all happened five minutes ago. She was making a bad start lying here asleep while he was up and about and she felt furious with herself—and somehow furious with him too.

With a slight gesture of his head he indicated the bedside table.

"I've brought you a cup of tea."

"Oh . . . er . . . thank you." Lying back against the pillow, she was uneasily conscious of her nakedness under the sheet. "I suppose I should have brought tea in to you," she said wryly. "What time is it?"

"Six thirty. And just to get the record straight, I don't want you bringing tea to my bedroom in the mornings. This is the one and only time I'll be doing it for you, by the way. I thought you might like to know your luggage is here," he added, nodding toward her large suitcase, now reposing on a stool at the end of the bed.

"Oh, thanks. Mr. Hardy brought it, I suppose."

"No, I fetched it. I thought you might be pleased to have all your gear here when you got up. Did you manage all right last night?"

"Yes, of course. I . . . I slept in my slip," she lied, and crimsoned as she saw his glance go to the floor, where she'd dropped her slip when she'd wriggled out of it last night. "Thank you for your trouble."

"It was no bother. I wanted to go round to the resort in any case. . . . I'm going to take a swim. You'd better drink your tea and wake up. I want you to make an early start this morning. There's a lot of work to catch up on, and the sooner I find out what you can—or can't—do, the better." He finished with a sardonic look.

Aidan didn't answer, though she was tempted to say something rude. When he'd gone, she sat up, holding the sheet over her naked breasts. Six thirty! He certainly believed in making an early start. At least it was something to know she didn't have to take him an early-morning cup of tea as she'd always done for Sylvia. But she certainly didn't want him coming into her room while she slept. It was only by good luck just now that her body had been covered by the sheet.

She reached for the tea. It was strong and black and very sweet. Ugh! Just the way she didn't like it. She drank it, shuddering slightly and wondering how he'd liked the medium rare steak she'd served him last night. He'd eaten it, it was true, but then, she was drinking the tea. Neither of them had the least idea of the other's tastes in anything. Including secretaries, she thought ironically, remembering his annoyance when she'd asked what his taste in secretaries was. She knew that Diane had been a lot older than she was and apparently much more sophisticated, and she wondered uneasily why she'd gone back to England.

Her tea finished, she got out of bed. It occurred to her that just possibly Guy had been offering an olive branch in fetching her luggage for her. He'd certainly been rude to her yesterday—unbearably so—and he was lucky she'd agreed to stay. Yet perhaps he'd been tired and hungry, she thought charitably. Maybe the storm in the air had affected him, maybe things had been going badly with his book. She knew how moody Sylvia could be when things weren't going well. She'd had to practically tiptoe around the house and make herself invisible until the tide turned and the good stuff started rolling in again.

Naked, she crossed the room and went into the bathroom. When she'd splashed her face she came back and opened her suitcase. He hadn't invited her, but she'd take a swim too, she decided. She'd make it an opportunity to apologise and start afresh. Perhaps things would work out well after all. She found her bikini and got into it quickly. It was emerald green, and as she fastened the tiny bra top she looked at herself critically in the big heart-shaped mirror above the dressing table. The green of the bikini sparked off the hidden fires in her grey eyes, but otherwise, she decided ruefully, the scanty covering did nothing for her. She hadn't been on the beach for about two months, what with her aunt's illness and death, and her tan had faded. She'd lost weight as well so that her never large breasts looked smaller than ever. She certainly wasn't voluptuous, and she was quite sure there'd be no sexy look in Guy Desailley's eyes when she appeared on his private beach in a few minutes' time.

Not that she wanted him to look at her that way, she

thought in annoyance as she turned away from her reflection and the sight of her suddenly flushed cheeks. She was here to work for him, not to try to stimulate his—his sexual appetite. To work for him and force him to take back the derogatory remarks he'd made about her yesterday. She brushed her hair vigorously and braided it at one side, securing the end with an elastic band, then, having found her surf towel and decided against sandals, she hurried through the house and down to the beach. Guy was already leaving the water as she came through the palms. He looked handsome and virile in minuscule black trunks as he waded through the shallows onto the white sand, his tanned body gleaming and wet. The air was warm, the light still soft, and Aidan swung her towel and planned the words of apology she meant to offer him. He was standing half turned away from her, a thoughtful expression on his face, his mouth slightly twisted. He was really almost too handsome, she thought. His body was superb and his black, curling hair sent shivers along her spine.

On the point of calling out to him, she suddenly wondered if he was thinking about his work and if she was intruding. She'd made up her mind to retreat when he turned slightly and saw her, and with a shrug, she walked toward him, dropping her towel and feeling unexpectedly self-conscious. His eyes looked a brighter blue in the sunlight, and she was strongly aware of his unconcealed appraisal of her.

"I thought I'd take a swim too," she said unnecessarily. "I hope I'm not interrupting your thoughts."

"No. I was thinking about you, actually," he said screwing up his eyes slightly.

Aidan flushed. When someone says something like that to you, you can't just continue on into the water and float off unconcernedly—particularly when that someone is your employer. So she stayed where she was, poking at the sand with one foot, then raising her eyes to ask him huskily, "Have you changed your mind about giving me a trial?"

"No," he said flatly. "That's still on. I'm not in the habit of changing my mind at a moment's notice."

Their eyes met briefly and once again she looked down at her feet. "I guess I should apologise for the way I acted yesterday. I shouldn't have lost my head . . . been so rude . . ."

"Oh forget it," he said with a shrug, and she sent him a swift look. How could he be so casual about the trauma of their first meeting? And about her apology, which had cost her at least a small effort. Did he think she was the only one who'd been at fault? Wasn't he going to admit he'd been decidedly rude and abrupt himself, since she'd come here in good faith? Apparently not, and since that was so . . . "How long am I to have to prove myself?" she asked. "You didn't make that clear."

He ran his fingers through his damp hair. "I'm not going to set arbitrary limits. In the long run, it could depend on how well we tolerate each other."

He flicked her a critical look as he spoke, and an unexpected antagonism ignited in her, so that it was all she could do not to tell him she didn't think she'd be able to tolerate him for more than a couple of hours at the most. She even resented the way he was looking at her, taking in her near-naked form quite openly, from head to foot. He'd called her a pretty girl yesterday, but no doubt he was modifying his opinion now that he saw her stripped. She longed to snatch up her towel and cover herself, or to run past him and submerge herself in the beautiful blue-green waters of the sea, but she stood as though petrified while his eyes roamed over her at their pleasure.

"You must try to put a little more fat on your bones

while you're here, Aidan," he told her at last, raising his eyes to hers and smiling slightly,

She stared at him speechlessly, her emotions in utter chaos. She was furious and yet—the way he'd spoken, the way he'd said her name, his voice soft, actually *soft*, had done something indescribable to her. Something that she resented.

"I'm not interested in putting fat on my bones," she flung at him. "And I don't expect to do so, running around for you."

"It was your choice," he reminded her with mocking reasonableness. "And now I'm going in to have some breakfast. If you want a swim, then have it, but don't take all day." Once more he raked his fingers through his black hair and strode away.

Aidan looked after him, her eyes dwelling on his muscular legs, his narrow hips, the richness of the tan he'd acquired, presumably in Spain. Somehow now that he'd gone, she didn't want to swim after all; she'd lost interest. And that was because she knew it was time to get ready for work, she told herself firmly, as she retraced her steps and picked up her towel. Along by the jetty she'd noticed a small cabin cruiser with its attendant dinghy. *His* boats, presumably, although he might just have hired them, of course.

In the bungalow she showered and then got into jeans, a yellow singlet top and flat-heeled sandals. She tidied her bed and did some unpacking before going out to have breakfast. She could smell coffee, and in the breakfast room off the kitchen she found Guy already sitting at the table, which was covered with a green and white checked cloth.

"I don't know what you like for your breakfast," he remarked as she came in to join him. "Eggs? Toast? Diane generally had muesli—there's a heap of it left in a jar somewhere if you fancy it."

"I'll find it," Aidan said and proceeded to do so. When she came back to the table she said conversationally, "Diane was your secretary, wasn't she?"

"That's right," he agreed. "Pass your cup and I'll pour you some coffee."

Aidan sat down opposite him, aware of a feeling of nervousness. She wasn't used to breakfasting with a man—particularly not with a handsome man who wore blue jeans and nothing else except a gold chain around his neck.

"What happened to her—To Diane?" she asked, to cover up her unease. She poured milk on her muesli and took the cup that he'd filled with delicious-smelling coffee.

He looked at her quizzically. "Nothing happened to her. Did you imagine I'd drowned her or strangled her or something like that?"

She coloured fiercely. "Of course not. I don't have that kind of mind. I'm not silly enough to imagine you live out the stories you write. I just wondered why she'd left, that's all—if she found you hard to get on with," she added, and then wished she hadn't.

"Diane worked for me for three years and believe it or not, she loved every minute of it," he told her with a crooked smile. "But last week she had news that her mother is in hospital in London, seriously ill. Does that answer your question?"

She writhed at his tone. "Yes. . . . I'm sorry. About her mother, I mean. Will she . . . will Diane come back?"

"I very much doubt it. She didn't adapt well to the heat. It was her first real experience of it. We never stayed in Spain in the summer. I'm afraid we've parted company for good."

"For good? That hardly seems fair," Aidan protested. He shrugged and poured himself another coffee and then sat back in his chair and looked at her impatiently. "After all, you're not going to live on this island permanently, are you? Shay said . . ." She stopped abruptly at the expression on his face.

"Well, carry on. What did Shay say? You two girls must have had quite a chat about me."

"We didn't, actually," Aidan said, annoyed to find herself blushing furiously. "But she did mention that you intended to buy a house in Sydney. And it would hardly be too hot for Diane there, would it?" she rushed on.

"Probably not." He looked at her quizzically. "However, I don't intend to spend the rest of my life working in cool climates to suit my secretary, if that's what you're propounding. I'm planning to do some travel in the outback during the next few years, and in case it hasn't struck you, I employ a secretary for my own benefit. If she can't fit into my life-style, then I have no use for her. You might do well to keep that in mind if you're so eager to prove yourself the ideal secretary," he concluded sardonically and got up from his chair. "I'll expect you to be ready to start work in half an hour."

"I'll be ready," Aidan said. She spoke calmly but her heart was hammering. She found him a most infuriating man. She might be eager to show him she was the perfect secretary, but that didn't mean she was the slightest bit interested in becoming a permanent fixture in his life or in fitting into his life-style. *She* would never last out three years. In fact, she suspected she might stay just long enough to make him eat his words and then she'd disappear as fast as she could.

Although at the rate she was going, it was going to take a very long time before he *would* eat his words, she reflected wryly.

She finished her breakfast and then washed the

dishes quickly, aware that this was part of her duties, though he hadn't told her so. She had to admit that he'd fixed his own breakfast and made coffee for her as well. That was at least one point in his favour, she thought as she cleaned her teeth at the bathroom basin. She reapplied lipstick and considered her reflection in the mirror. She didn't look too bad now that she was fully dressed. But there she went again, the typical female, ever conscious of her appearance. As if he cared about that!

In the room that was her office she uncovered the typewriter, put out a pile of paper and adjusted the height of the chair to suit herself. She was glancing over the reference books on the shelves when Guy came in.

"Type these pages for me, Aidan," he said, scarcely looking at her. "I'd like to get some idea of your capabilities. If you have any problems, any queries about anything whatsoever, save them up until later when I'm free. I want to see what you can do on your own without interrupting me every ten minutes or so expecting me to do your work for you. You're the one who's being paid to interpret my scribbles and to make clean, readable copies for me to edit. I've a whole stack of work waiting to be done. Diane did practically nothing the last couple of weeks she was here, so I hope you're not going to be wilting in the heat."

"I certainly hope I won't be. You're very unsympathetic, aren't you?"

"Don't tell me your heart's bleeding for Diane. Her bad luck could be your good fortune. It may interest you to know she had a weight problem. To keep her figure the way she liked it, she had to diet constantly, which can contribute quite drastically to dehydration. That sort of thing won't bother you, that's for sure," he finished with a slow glance over her slim figure.

"Though if I might offer a word of advice, I'd suggest you wear dresses or skirts instead of those jeans. They'll allow the air to circulate over your body more freely and help your cooling system."

"Thank you," Aidan said, forcing a smile. "I might take your advice, though I see you don't follow it yourself," she added, glancing at his tightly trousered legs.

"I'm able to go topless, Miss Elliot," he said mockingly. He switched on the ceiling fan as he left the room and then looked back from the doorway to tell her, "Keep the fan going while you're working. That way you'll cope better while you're getting acclimatised."

"Thank you," she said again. She settled herself at her desk, looking at the top sheet of the wad of pages he'd given her. At first glance it looked like some sort of a puzzle. Great chunks of type were scored out and written over in black ink, and the margins were crowded with inserts and notes. His handwriting was certainly not easy to decipher, but neither had Sylvia's been. It was just a matter of getting used to it, of interpreting squiggles at the end of words and discovering what symbols he used, she told herself optimistically.

She'd barely settled down to work when the telephone rang, and she hurried to answer it.

"Aidan? This is Vanda Hardy, from the resort. I'm ringing in case Guy's forgotten to remind you to put your order in before eleven."

"Order? What order?" Aidan asked, bewildered.

"For groceries, fruit, vegetables, meat. Anything at all you want from the mainland," Vanda Hardy said. Aidan guessed from her voice that she was more likely to be Brian Hardy's daughter than his wife. "It's a weekly service, so get it sorted out, will you? I'm sure Guy will give you some help with it."

Aidan grimaced. She couldn't see herself interrupting Guy to ask him to help her make up the weekly order. She'd have to manage on her own, and it would be just too bad for him if she missed anything he wanted especially. "I'll ring you back, Vanda," she promised, then asked, "Are you Mr. Hardy's daughter?"

A soft laugh came over the wires. "That's right. I expect Guy's mentioned me to you. How are you coping over there, anyhow? My father said you looked like a chicken about to be thrown into the duck pond."

Aidan winced. Had she appeared as apprehensive as that? She didn't really think so. However . . . "I've managed to scramble ashore," she said dryly. "But I'd better go and fix up that order."

"Do that. When you phone back, just give it to whoever answers. It's not my responsibility. Just a friendly gesture. You must come across to the resort sometime when you're free. It's only a short walk through the garden. Bring your swimming gear. We have a lovely pool, and you'll meet some nice people."

"Thanks, I'd like that," Aidan said, surprised and warmed by the invitation.

"Oh—and before you go—don't overorder, will you? Guy mightn't have told you that he eats over here at night quite often. Good-bye for now. I'll be seeing you, Aidan."

Aidan hung up. You learn something every day, she thought as she went out to the kitchen. But you didn't learn it from Guy Desailley.

It was another hour before she started to work, and she found it very hard going. The pages he'd given her weren't the start of the book, and she didn't have a clear idea what it was all about, which didn't help matters. As for his writing—she'd always prided herself on her ability to decipher difficult handwriting, but this was certainly a tax on her ingenuity. She did her best with it, but she had to leave several gaps, which was frustrating. If she could have consulted Guy just a couple of times, it would have made all the difference.

As the morning went by she could feel the perspiration trickling down between her breasts, and she was uncomfortably hot in her jeans. Guy had been quite right about wearing loose clothing, and at last she went into her bedroom and changed into a loose cotton dress, having first taken off her bra as well as the jeans and T-shirt. She dispensed with a belt, and feeling much more comfortable, she went out to the kitchen for a long, cold drink, which she carried onto the front verandah.

To her amazement, she saw Guy lounging on the beach. He wore white swimming trunks and sunglasses, and he was smoking. Aidan felt furious. Since he wasn't working, he could have given her a little help, but obviously he was determined to prove that she wasn't as smart as she'd claimed to be.

Well, she was equally determined to prove that she was, and finishing her drink, she went briskly back to her office and applied herself to the task of filling in all those blanks with something, guessing what she couldn't make out, and scribbling a pencilled query over a word here, a phrase there.

The afternoon was almost over by the time she'd finished all the work he'd given her. She hadn't eaten any lunch and she had no idea whether he'd had any or not and she really didn't care. She made herself a tomato sandwich and helped herself to fruit juice. It wasn't the kind of meal that was likely to fatten her, but she wasn't going to risk dehydration through going without. As she ate her sandwich she remembered the order she'd telephoned through to the resort. She hadn't had a chance to check with Guy, and if she'd missed out on any essentials, then that was too bad. She wasn't a mind reader nor did she have a crystal ball.

Her meal finished, she went to her bedroom, brushed out her hair and replaited it and then put on a belt and her sandals. She could hear Guy typing away in his study, but since she'd finished the work he'd left her to do, she felt she was within her rights in taking an hour or so off. *He'd* had plenty of time off this morning. Leaving by the back door, she made her way through the garden to a track that led in the general direction of the resort.

It was a pleasant walk in the shade of the tall trees and palms, though the air was still and humid. The breeze from the water didn't reach here but at least it was shady, and as she walked she began to realise that this must once have been part of a huge tropical garden. There were frangipani and hibiscus flowers in profusion. A small wooden bridge crossed a little stream where the water came down from the hillside to find its way to the sea. Huge mango trees overhung the path, and the green fruit on their long stalks made the trees look like something decorative from a ballet set. Poincianas dripped with red-gold flowers, and there were butterflies everywhere. It was a tropical Eden.

Aidan picked a huge peach-pink frangipani flower and tucked it into her hair above one ear, inhaling its rich, seductive fragrance. She strolled on, humming. Some way ahead through the leafy greenness she saw a white wood gate and beyond that a sweep of lawn. The resort! Already she could hear voices, and then she caught a glimpse of the thatched roofs of the guest units and her heartbeat quickened. She had the curious feeling that she'd been shut up with Guy Desailley for a week instead of for a day, and she longed to see other people, to talk to them. Perhaps she'd see if she could find Vanda Hardy, though it was a little late for social visits from her point of view. There was dinner to cook, after all. . . . Still, when she reached the gate the temptation to go through was too great to resist, and a minute later she was on the gravel path on the other side. Glancing back at the notice at the side of the gate, she read, Private Property No Admittance. She shrugged. Who'd want to enter to be greeted—or otherwise—by a domineering, disagreeable author? She wandered on along the path that led across a lawn scattered with banana plants, coconut palms and great clumps of brightly coloured flowers. To the right was the beach and ahead of her was a cluster of buildings, Polynesian in style, with steep wood roofs and big carved poles and beams. Nearby, the waters of a tiled swimming pool glinted blue and from there came shouts and laughter, and Aidan found herself unconsciously smiling.

Absentmindedly, she picked another frangipani flower and sniffed at it appreciatively, twirling it lightly between finger and thumb.

"Naughty, naughty! Mustn't pick the flowers," a male voice remarked, and she glanced round to see a husky young man smiling at her. He wore brief white shorts and a white T-shirt. His blond hair and blue eyes gleamed in the sunlight, and Aidan smiled back at him spontaneously. What a change he was from that dark-browed ogre at the bungalow!

"Have I committed a terrible sin?" she asked him laughingly, and he appraised her, his expression a mock-serious one.

"You have, but I shan't report you to the authorities, on certain conditions."

"And what would they be? Perhaps if I gave you this flower . . ."

He took it and then told her, "That's not payment

enough. But we'll discuss that later. I'm Steve Guerney, by the way. And you're . . . ?"

"Aidan Elliot."

"Hi, Aidan. You can't have been here long or I'd have spotted you before this. When did you arrive?"

"Yesterday. But I'm not staying at the resort. I'm from . . . from next door."

"Next door?" he repeated, then glanced beyond her shoulder. "Oh, you mean Private Property. No Admittance. Doesn't some writer bloke live there? Is he your . . ."

He paused and Aidan said, "My employer. Guy Desailley. You may have read some of his books." She glanced at her watch. "As a matter of fact, I should be going back now."

"Oh, but you can't disappear yet," Steve protested. "You haven't fulfilled those conditions. If you don't want to get into really serious trouble—and be locked up and fed bread and water for a week—then you must . . . um . . . agree to join me for a drink down by the pool."

She looked at him ruefully, badly tempted. But she knew that if she gave in, she was likely to be there for another hour, and though the penalty for that might not be to be locked up and fed bread and water for a week, it certainly wasn't going to endear her to Guy.

"Thank you, Steve. But I really can't. Not this afternoon. I just nipped off for a few minutes to stretch my legs. I ought to be going back now."

"Then let me come with you," he offered promptly.

"Okay," she agreed with a smile. "But you won't be able to come in. Mr. Desailley doesn't like intruders."

"Intruders? When I'm seeing you home? Is that how I'd be classed?"

"Probably," she admitted as they walked toward the

gate. "So don't expect to be invited in for a drink or to meet Mr. Desailley, if that's what you have in mind."

"It's not what I have in mind. This boss of yours sounds like a bit of a tyrant, though, Aidan." He opened the gate to let her through. "Is he?"

Aidan shrugged. Somehow she didn't feel inclined to air her views on Guy Desailley, so she changed the subject. "Where do you live, Steve?"

"In Brisbane. I'm a geologist. On three weeks' holiday up here—one of which has already gone." They walked on along the path together, their footsteps soundless on the fallen leaves and decaying vegetation of what was virtually a rain forest. "Is this man you work for married?"

She coloured faintly, a little disconcerted by his determination to talk about Guy. "No. Are you?"

He grinned. "No. And not thinking of it at the moment. So how about coming over tonight after dinner, and we can listen to some music or dance. You surely don't have to work at night."

"I just might have to. You see, I'm a sort of secretary plus. I have other things to do besides type manuscripts, so I can't be sure. Anyhow, I don't think I'd better make any arrangements for tonight, Steve. I only started here yesterday and I haven't really got the hang of things yet."

"Then tomorrow," he persisted, and when she murmured, "Maybe," he commented, "I'm beginning to think you're allergic to me."

"Of course I'm not. I'd like to spend the evening with you sometime, but we'll have to leave it for now." They had come in view of the bungalow and she slowed her footsteps. "I don't think you'd better come any further, Steve."

"Then how do I get in touch with you?"

She bit her lip. She didn't like to suggest the telephone, and eventually she told him, "Let's make it tomorrow afternoon about this time—at the gate. We can arrange something then."

"Okay," he agreed, brightening, and reached out to take her hand briefly in his. "I'll see you then, Aidan. Don't forget!"

"I won't," she promised and, turning away, hurried on toward the bungalow. She entered by the back door and then went quietly through the house to see if Guy was still working in his study.

He was, and she breathed a sigh of relief before hurrying to her room. There she switched on the ceiling fan and flung herself down on the bed for a few minutes' rest.

She was almost asleep when Guy's voice roused her.

"So you're back. Where the devil did you disappear to earlier?"

Chapter Three

She sat up abruptly, pushing her hair back from her face. She was perspiring, and what she wanted most of all was a cool shower. The frangipani she'd tucked into her hair had fallen bruised and sweet-smelling onto the sheet, and she picked it up and hid it in her hand as though there was some guilt attached to it.

"I went for a walk through the garden. Isn't that allowed?"

"Through the garden?" He leaned one hand against the wall and looked at her darkly, his bare chest gleaming, his hair ruffled, his eyes narrowed. "You mean to the resort, I suppose. I was wondering how long it would be before you disappeared in that direction."

"Were you? Well, now you know," she said, rather rudely. She slipped her bare feet to the floor and stood up. He *was* a tyrant, she reflected. Steve was quite

55

right. He stood glaring down at her as if he had the right to order her every movement. She was mad, in fact, to be working for him. She went to the mirror, and as she replaited her mussed hair she looked at him through the glass and told him, "Vanda Hardy asked me to go over some time when I spoke to her on the phone this morning—about your order. You didn't think to mention that to me, did you?"

He ignored the question and watched her steadily, his eyes, she was certain, taking in the fact that she wore no bra. "Vanda nominated this afternoon specifically, did she?"

"Not exactly." She coloured slightly, and to escape his raking gaze, turned to find her sandals and slip her feet into them. "But it suited me to go when I did." She straightened up and looked at him fully, her grey eyes cool. "Surely I don't have to ask your permission before I put one foot in front of the other. I'm not a slave, you know. You haven't bought me."

"I wouldn't make an offer for you if I had the opportunity," he said, his lips quirking in a sardonic smile. "But next time you think of vanishing, you might find out if it suits *me*. You should have been here this afternoon to take delivery of that order you put through. Your common sense should have told you that. As it was, I had to interrupt my work to do what I'm paying you to do—which is to see to all the extraneous matters that interfere with my working day."

Aidan swallowed and had an inward struggle. What he said was quite right, and she knew now that she should have been there. But Vanda hadn't told her when her order would arrive, and she hadn't been smart enough to think about it herself. The trouble was that at Whale Beach she'd been used to jumping into

56

the car and whizzing off to do the week's shopping. She bit her lip with chagrin.

"I'm sorry," she said stiffly, and saw the line of his lips relax slightly. But apart from that he gave no sign that he'd even heard her apology.

"Did you finish the work I left you this morning?"

"To the best of my ability. Your writing has a few idiosyncrasies I haven't yet unravelled. If I'd known you were messing about on the beach this morning, I'd have had a word with you about some of your symbols and your abbreviations."

His lips had tightened again. "For your information, Miss Elliot, I was not messing about on the beach. You claim to have worked for a writer for four years. Don't you know that writers often spend some time thinking? Though perhaps your little old lady didn't have to do much of that with her simple stories for girls. . . . Now let's see what kind of a job you've done."

He strode through to the office, and she followed him after one swift glance in the mirror that showed her flaming cheeks and eyes sparked with fire. She really didn't know what had got into her. She'd never have thought of speaking to Sylvia the way she'd spoken to him. But then, Sylvia had never provoked her.

In the office he was already leafing through the typing she'd done and she told him coldly, "I'd rather you didn't come into my bedroom, by the way. Particularly without knocking."

He looked up swiftly. "I knocked, Miss Elliot. But you were asleep. What's bothering you anyhow? Do you imagine I had any purpose other than stirring you up and getting you back on the job? Or are you one of those females who always have sex on their minds?"

Her face flamed. "Who said I have sex on my mind?"

"What else were you worried about, then?" he

asked, his mouth twisting. "Obviously you suspect that I had some ulterior motive in coming to your room. I assure you I hadn't. As far as I'm concerned, you're my secretary and nothing else. I'd infinitely prefer to keep sex out of our relationship."

"That will suit me," she retorted, and added on the spur of the moment, "I have a boyfriend in Sydney, as it happens, and I'm perfectly satisfied with him." She actually thought of Robert as she spoke, and though she wasn't in the least interested in marrying him, at this moment he seemed so infinitely preferable to the man who now confronted her, she almost persuaded herself that breaking their engagement had been a mistake.

Guy looked at her sharply, taking no more interest in the papers in his hand. "Then if that's so, why did you rush to take a position all the way up here?"

She widened her eyes. "You don't intend to live here, do you? I understood you mean to go to Sydney. And I wanted to help Shay," she improvised.

"So you came out of motives that were purely noble. You made a personal sacrifice on behalf of both myself and Shay," he mocked. "Is that it?"

She coloured. "I didn't say that. I needed a change, and that was a big factor in helping me make up my mind."

"A change?" He leaned against her desk and looked at her levelly. "I thought you'd spent the whole of your working life doing more or less what you're supposed to be doing here."

"Yes, but since my . . . Miss Barrett died, I've been responsible for settling her affairs, for getting her house ready for sale. It's been . . . difficult. I wanted a change from that."

"How did you come to have such responsibilities?" he wanted to know.

"Because I lived with Miss Barrett. If you must know, she was my aunt."

"I see," he said after a moment. He tapped the papers against his thigh, and when he spoke again his tone was softer. "I didn't realise that Miss Barrett's death was a personal loss. I'm sorry. And the house—it means you have no home now. It wasn't left to you?"

"No," she admitted. "My aunt left most of her estate to an organisation that works for children. The house is to be sold to raise money for it. Shay and I were her only close relatives. She left me a little money, but the house is old, it needs a lot of renovations and repairs. I love it but . . ." She stopped, thinking she was talking too much and that he wouldn't want to hear, but he waited for her to go on. "Well, Aunt Sylvia thought—knew"—she amended quickly—"I was going to marry Robert."

"The boyfriend you mentioned. He's well off, then?"

She nodded, hating to have to go on with the lie, but not seeing what else she could do. "He works for his father's architectural firm."

"And when's the wedding to be?"

"We haven't decided," she said shortly and changed the subject. "Are you satisfied with my work, Mr. Desailley? I've left no gaps but I've made quite a few guesses. I'd have done better if you'd done me the courtesy of giving me a briefing this morning."

"Are you trying to teach me how I should treat my secretary?" he demanded.

"I suppose I am," she admitted with a cool smile. "If you want to get the best out of me, then it would help if you'd done what I said. But perhaps you'd prefer to prove the validity of your original judgment of me— that I'm no use to you."

He gave her a thoughtful stare. "I'll pass judgment on you later. Meanwhile, you can pack away that box of stuff in the kitchen. And there are a couple of letters I want you to type for me too. I've made a rough draft of what I want, and you'll have to work from that. If you'd been here, I'd have dictated to you."

Aidan had apologised once, and she wasn't apologising again.

"About dinner," she said politely. "When would you like me to prepare it? Before I do the letters, or afterward?"

"I won't be in for dinner tonight."

"You won't! Then I wish you'd let me know earlier," she exclaimed, thinking that she could have spent the evening with Steve Guerney if she'd known she would be free. Instead, she'd be here at the bungalow on her own—with the letters.

He looked at her coldly. "You're too quick with your tongue, Miss Elliot. The result of working for a relative, I daresay. I'll tell you my plans when it suits me and you can fit in with them. Is that clear?"

"Perfectly clear," she said, tight-lipped and angry. "Now I really know where I stand."

"Good," he said, and left the room.

It was just getting dark, and she'd finished typing the letters when she heard the motor of his boat as he left the jetty. She went onto the verandah and watched the light moving over the water. He could have asked her if she'd like a lift round to the resort, she thought resentfully. His letters weren't all that important, surely. But no, he preferred to treat her as some very lowly kind of employee, which was hardly fair since they were in such an unusual and isolated situation.

She wished she'd arranged something with Steve now. She didn't feel like making her way through the darkness of the tropical garden to the resort grounds, and besides, by this time, Steve might have found someone else to spend the evening with. All in all, she felt rather woebegone and badly done by.

Inside, she made herself a salad and a pot of tea and carried them out to the front verandah. Outside was only the dark sea with that one light she'd noticed the night before. The sound of the waves was no more than a whisper, and the soft *click-clack* of the palm leaves was nerve-racking in her present state of mind.

She ate her meal without appetite and washed the dishes, reflecting that life at the moment seemed to consist largely in doing domestic chores in splendid isolation. What girl in her right mind would ever dream of travelling more than 2,000 kilometres for this?

In the sitting room she found a stack of old records, and she played one or two, mostly to relieve the silence. Then, restlessly, while the music was still playing, she wandered through the house, switching on the lights as she went. At the door of Guy's bedroom she lingered, looking inside curiously. The bed was made, a blue silk dressing gown was draped over a chair, and there was a fresh herbal smell of after-shave. She moved away moodily and went outside. How long would it be before he came home, she wondered?

The moon had risen and the beach was washed in light. The sea shone like metal, the leaves of the palms moved softly. What a marvellously romantic place to come to for a honeymoon, she thought unexpectedly. Or with a lover. She'd never had a lover. Robert, when they were engaged, had never asked her to sleep with him, and she didn't really know much about passion. She just hadn't met a man yet who had swept away her inhibitions, aroused passionate desire in her.

They were disturbing thoughts, and they reminded her uncomfortably of the question Guy had asked her earlier: Are you one of those females with sex forever on her mind? She wasn't, and yet now . . .

She kicked off her sandals and ran across the sand, feeling it cool and squeaky under her bare feet, but it wasn't as easy as that to escape from her thoughts. What was *he* doing at this moment, she wondered. Dancing? Making love? She began to splash moodily along in the shallow water, pulling her hair loose from its braid, tossing it about her face. She was quite sure *he* knew all there was to know about passion and lovemaking. It was a wonder he hadn't married again. Whatever else she felt about him, she had to admit that he was an attractive and virile man. But perhaps he'd never got over the loss of his wife, or possibly he'd never met another woman who reached the standard of perfection she'd set. He didn't seem to have a very high opinion of women at all events, judging from his attitude toward her. And no matter what he said, she thought his resignation to the loss of Diane was indicative of cruel indifference. Diane had worked for him for three years, and apparently she'd been satisfactory in every way. Yet he wasn't prepared to make a single compromise in order to make it easier for her to stay on.

Immersed in her thoughts, Aidan suddenly found herself thigh deep in the water, the skirt of her dress drenched. With a swift movement she pulled the loose cotton garment over her head and tossed it onto the sand; then, wearing only her panties, she waded out into the sea. The moonlight shone on her breasts; little silver leaves of light danced in her eyes. She submerged herself in the softly caressing water and then turned to float on her back and stare up at the silvery moon floating in the limpid sky as she was floating in the sea. Her hair, loosened from its braid, drifted around her head and she felt the utmost bliss. All that was needed to make it perfect was someone to share her pleasure. Someone . . .

She closed her eyes and tried to conjure up an image

of Steve, but no matter how hard she concentrated her thoughts on blond hair and friendly blue eyes, Guy's face persistently superimposed itself: the firm jaw darkened with stubble, the thick, curling black hair rumpled, the eyes—midnight blue—inscrutable, examining hers as if they'd find their way through to her very soul. . . .

Something made her open her eyes, and she turned on her side, groping with her feet for the sand, aware of a light moving along the jetty, of the figure of a man in white shirt and dark pants, flashing a torch ahead of him. It was Guy! Aidan's stomach churned as the realisation of her near-nakedness struck her. What on earth was she to do? She thought wildly of dashing out of the water, racing across the beach and through the trees to the safety of the bungalow, and then common sense came surging back. She didn't have to do that. She didn't have to do a thing. All she need do was to stay where she was and pray that he wouldn't see her. And even if he did, she didn't have to leave the water.

She moved silently and cautiously away from the shore until the water was deep enough to cover all of her except her head, keeping her eyes fixed on Guy's moving figure as she did so. He was walking quickly; already he'd reached the end of the jetty and was starting across the beach. She was thankful she hadn't acted on impulse, and she watched with relief as he disappeared into the shadow of the palms. Presently she saw more lights shining from the bungalow.

Shivering, though not with cold, she plunged through the water and waded onto the sand. Where on earth was her dress? Panic rose in her and she began to run, covering her naked breasts with her hands as though to hide them. Then with a little gasp she saw the sodden garment lying at the very edge of the water. She pounced on it, shaking it out with trembling fingers so that she could pull it over her head, shuddering as it clung to her dripping body, damp and sandy and uncomfortable.

She was pressing her wet hair back from her face when she discovered she was not alone. Guy stood no more than two yards away and in the moonlight she caught the glitter of his dark eyes. She drew a sharp breath.

"What do you want?" she demanded huskily, sure that he'd seen her struggling into her clothes, and hating him for it.

He came several steps closer. "I was looking for you. Are you all right, Aidan?"

"You don't have to worry about me," she retorted, and heard him draw a breath of impatience.

"You weren't at the lodge, you weren't in the bungalow. It's surely natural that I should want to find you. . . . What have you been doing? Skinny-dipping, by the look of you. Or were you trying to drown yourself?"

"I haven't been driven to that yet," she said, wrapping her arms around herself. "I wanted a swim, that's all. It was hot in the house."

"It's certainly pleasanter outside," he agreed, and she thought she saw his mouth curving as his eyes moved over her, bedraggled in her clinging dress, her hair hanging round her face and dripping wetly onto her shoulders. "It's a beautiful night. Look at those stars—so big and bright and close to the earth. It reminds me of Spain without the music. . . . I suppose you haven't been to Spain, Aidan."

"No," she said, hugging herself harder, wondering why on earth she stood here listening to him when all she wanted was to get away from him. "I've never been out of Australia."

"Well, you're young. You've plenty of time for

travel. Maybe you'll go overseas for your honeymoon, as your cousin Shay did."

She didn't answer. She didn't want to talk about her fictitious honeymoon; instead she asked him acidly, "Did you enjoy yourself at the resort tonight?"

She saw his dark brows rise. "What's the bitter note in your voice meant to indicate?"

"If you really want to know—that you could have asked me if I'd like a lift over there instead of leaving me here on my own. But I suppose in your opinion, secretaries are barely human," she finished, and was appalled at herself. She sounded even to her own ears like a neglected wife or mistress.

"Oh, for God's sake," he exclaimed, "If there's something you want, you can ask for it, can't you? You do have a tongue in your head—which you've been only too willing to use during the short time I've known you."

"You didn't give me a chance to ask anything," she snapped. "But forget it. It doesn't matter." She turned away and began to walk past him, but his hand shot out and he pulled her toward him and glared down at her.

"What's got into you, for heaven's sake? Are you missing your boyfriend? If so . . ."

"If so, what?" she breathed, twisting away from him with a fierce movement, all too aware of the electric effect his touch was having on her.

He pulled her back to him, his arms closing about her and bringing her body hard against his own, so that she felt his warmth come through to her cool, wet flesh. The thumping of his heart was almost audible.

"If so, perhaps I can help."

He tilted her face up, his fingers under her chin, and his mouth found hers. He kissed her hotly in a way she'd never been kissed before, his arms holding her closely, inescapably, yet almost protectively. Her pulses raced, and she didn't pull away. It was almost as though she'd been mesmerised. Besides—besides, she was swooningly aware of a sensual delight as their lips clung and the blood ran fast through her veins.

When his mouth moved slowly to the corner of her own, then down to her throat, she tilted her head back, closing her eyes, her fingers going of their own accord to the hair that grew thick and curling at the back of his head. She had the feeling she never wanted to move— she was content to be here forever, his body warm against her own, his breath touching her throat and then coming to her temple, his voice murmuring against her ear something that she couldn't even interpret.

She was scarcely conscious of what was happening when she sank down with him onto the sand to lie there, her legs entwined with his, his mouth once more moving sensuously against her lips. Once, she opened her eyes but the moonlight made her dizzy and she closed them again to go back to her dream. His lips left hers to stroke down her cheek to her neck. He made no attempt to push the material of her dress out of his way as his fingers stroked her flesh through the softness of the fabric.

It seemed an eternity before he finally drew away from her gently to sit up, half turned away from her. Aidan lay where she was for a long moment, feeling cool at the removal of his body, feeling a strange sense of loss. Her senses were confused and she found it difficult to come back to reality.

Then, without turning his head, he asked her in a matter-of-fact voice, "Are you feeling comforted, Miss Elliot?"

Comforted? At that word she seemed to spring to defensive life again. Comforted! He was thinking of Robert, of course, while for her . . . Robert had never been so far from her mind. She was aware of a sense of outrage—of having been forced into something against her will. Yet how could she protest now when she hadn't protested before? When she'd been so compliant, allowing him to do as he pleased? Which wasn't, she realised with a slight shock, very much. Or wouldn't seem so to him.

She scrambled to her feet, feeling undignified, bewildered, and very conscious of the fact that this was a situation she couldn't handle because she didn't understand her own reactions. He, Guy, might imagine she was pretending he was Robert, but that was so far from the truth it was ludicrous. Then who had she been pretending he was? Why had she been so unresisting, so passively responsive, if there were such a thing? She couldn't understand it herself, and she quite simply didn't know what to do.

He got slowly to his feet and stood beside her, but he didn't touch her. She turned her head and met his eyes in the moonlight and then looked quickly away again. She couldn't see any future for herself as his secretary if she were going to let this kind of thing happen, particularly in view of the fact that he'd said specifically, "We'll keep sex out of our relationship."

"I'm cold," she said, feeling the sandy dampness of her skirt against her bare legs. "I . . . I want to go inside."

"Very wise," he said. He put his arm across her shoulders and she drew away from him quickly.

"Don't touch me. And don't . . . don't ever do that again."

His arm fell to his side but he kept pace with her as she hurried toward the bungalow, her teeth chattering with nervousness.

"Don't make too much of what's just happened, Aidan," he said maddeningly. "I shan't hold it against you. You were obviously badly in need of comforting, and though you mightn't think so, I have a fairly soft heart where women are concerned. Unfortunately."

A soft heart! It was all she could do to stop herself from laughing derisively. As for being comforted, she'd never been more shaken.

"I don't believe you have a heart at all," she muttered. "And if you have, I'm not interested."

"I should think not," he mocked. "After all, you're a respectably engaged girl. Isn't that so?"

She didn't answer, but hurried up the steps ahead of him and sought the sanctuary of her own room.

She didn't know how she was going to face him the next morning. The incident on the beach had upset her badly. His kisses had disturbed her so much that she'd scarcely slept, and she was haunted by the fear that she might lose her head over him, which would be totally disastrous.

She was up early in the morning, and having checked that he wasn't on the beach, she got into her bikini and went down for a quick swim. If he joined her, she thought, it would be his choice and not hers. But he didn't come, though she encountered him when she went back to the bungalow, wrapped up in her towelling robe.

"I hope that early morning dip has cleared your head, Aidan," he told her. "There's a good few hours of work in store for you today. You didn't make a bad job at all of that little lot you struggled through yesterday, though there are one or two things I want to discuss with you this morning."

She flashed him a quick glance. "You mean you're actually going to take my advice?"

"I mean I actually am," he agreed ironically. "So you can congratulate yourself, Miss Elliot. You've scored a point." His glance went to her lips as he spoke, and she moistened them nervously, thinking helplessly of what had happened on the beach last night, and sure that he must be thinking of it too. She could have died of embarrassment, and just looking at him sent shivers along her nerves. Reminding herself fiercely that he'd told her—*warned* her—not to make too much of it, she brushed past him with an abrupt movement.

"Excuse me. I'm going in to dress. But while I think of it, I'd like to know if you'll be wanting lunch today. And if you'll be in to dinner tonight."

A brief expression of annoyance crossed his face, and then he told her, "You can bring me in a sandwich and coffee at two o'clock. And yes, I'll be in to dinner. Does that satisfy you?"

She stared back at him baffled, her cheeks slowly colouring. Just what was he implying by that question?

"I can arrange my day better if I know what's ahead of me," she said stiffly.

"Then that's the important thing, isn't it?" he said sardonically.

It wasn't until she was in her room dressing that she worked out what he meant by that, and then she was furious with herself—and with him. He thought she was acting as if *she* were the important one, demanding to know his plans for the day.

All in all, she wasn't really surprised when she took his sandwich in to him at two o'clock to find he wasn't there, and to discover he'd gone out in the boat. So whether or not he'd be in to dinner tonight was anyone's guess, and she would have learned a lesson.

She ate her own lunch and went back to work. Diane had certainly left a lot of unfinished business behind her, but now that she'd had some cooperation and guidance from Guy, she was better able to handle the work. She found his writing tough, clever stuff— concise and graphic, with touches of wry, sophisticated

69

humour. It didn't appeal to her feminine mind particularly, but she admired wholeheartedly his ability to intrigue and to convey reality, and the reason for his success seemed obvious.

She heard him come in sometime during the afternoon, but with an effort of will she kept on working, though the impulse to see him, to speak to him, to refresh her memory of him, was almost overpowering. Why, she didn't know. Or so she told herself.

An hour or so later, she could see from her window that the sky had darkened and clouds were beginning to roll in across the water. The humidity was oppressive and—despite her light, loose clothing, the movement of air caused by the ceiling fan, and frequent drinks of water—she was wilting. She needed a break, and besides, she'd promised to meet Steve. If she didn't go now, she'd be caught in the storm. She could hear Guy typing away in his study, and having put on her sandals and fastened a belt around her waist to cinch in the white cotton dress she was wearing, she left the house and made her way along the path to the resort.

Curiously, it was of Guy she thought and not of Steve as she hurried to her rendezvous. Her mind, freed of the pressure of work, went over and over what had taken place on the beach the night before, and her body tingled as she re-experienced Guy's embrace, the feel of his muscular hardness against her, his thighs against hers as their legs twined together. It all seemed impossibly unreal, yet she knew that she wanted to have it happen again. So what kind of a fool was she? To him it had meant nothing. Comfort, he'd called it, though somehow she found it impossible to believe it was as simple as that. He'd been carried away at least a little, she assured herself, though perhaps that was merely because he was a man with a passionate nature. Why hadn't he married again? she wondered, and a disturbing thought followed close on the heels of that question: Had he satisfied his need for sex, for a woman's body, with Diane? And despite his assertion that he wanted to keep sex out of their relationship, would he start looking to her, Aidan, to take Diane's place in that way too?

Well, he could look to her all he liked, she told herself, shocked by the direction her thoughts were taking. There'd be no more passionate interludes between them. She'd make sure of that in the future.

Steve was waiting for her when she reached the gate. Rather reluctantly, because of the threatening storm, she agreed to have a drink with him while they made plans for a further meeting. They'd barely settled themselves with their drinks at a poolside table, when Brian Hardy came by and stopped in his tracks, looking at her in surprise.

"Nice to see you here, Miss Elliot. Work finished for the day?"

"That's right," she told him with a bright smile. "I've earned a break."

"I'm sure you have. I hope you'll feel free to come over here any time you want to," he said genially and, smiling at both her and Steve, moved on.

Steve at once began to make plans for the evening. "Have dinner with me," he suggested, "and then we can dance, if you'd like that. There's live music tonight, I believe. A dance band's coming over from the mainland."

"That would be great, but I can't have dinner with you tonight," Aidan said, a little embarrassed. For some reason she didn't particularly want to spend the evening with Steve, but she could think of no good reason to refuse him. "I could come over to the dance for a while, though, unless it's raining. I just wouldn't be able to make it then."

Steve glanced up at the sky, which was now swarming with clouds.

"Oh, that storm will be over in an hour or so," he said confidently, putting down his glass and smiling at her in his friendly way. "Though if you've finished work for the day, do you need to go back next door at all? That dress you're wearing's okay, as far as I'm concerned."

"Oh, Steve!" she protested, laughing and glancing down at it. "It's a mess—I've had it on all day. At any rate, I have to cook dinner for my boss."

"Good lord, really? I thought you were doing typing or something like that."

"I am, but there are all sorts of other things I have to see to as well so he's free to concentrate on his work. It's what I'm paid for, and that's all there is to it." A few big drops of rain fell and she jumped to her feet. "I must fly. Don't bother coming to the gate with me, Steve."

"I'll come and pick you up at eight fifteen," he said, getting to his feet too.

"Well . . ." Aidan hesitated. She didn't particularly want Steve picking her up at the bungalow but neither did she like the idea of walking all that way in the dark alone. "All right," she agreed, and with a wave of her hand hurried away.

Chapter Four

She was drenched when she reached the bungalow, and she was in her bedroom changing out of her soaking dress when she heard Guy come into the office.

"Are you there, Aidan?"

"I'm in the bedroom," she called, hastily snatching up a pair of panties with one hand and groping for her robe with the other. Her hair was wet and she combed it back quickly and then went into the office. He was standing there, shirtless as usual, and she dragged her eyes from him unwillingly, and pretended to examine a paper on her desk.

"What have you been doing? Taking a shower? Or did you get caught in the storm?"

She shrugged and didn't answer directly. "I've been having a break. I think I've done my quota of work for the day. Or do you expect me to work till I collapse?"

His lips tightened and she could feel his forbidding glance on her though she didn't dare to raise her eyes.

"I'm not a slave driver. If you're satisfied with what you've done, then that's all right. I just wanted to tell you I'm taking the boat out to see if I can catch some fish for our dinner. If you were dressed, I'd have asked you to come along."

Her heart jumped and she felt a sharp pang of disappointment, but she said coolly, "Thank you. But I . . . I want to wash my hair. I'm going out after dinner." She raised her eyes to his face automatically as she spoke and then lowered them quickly as she met his dark blue gaze. A shaft of feeling shot through her.

"Oh? To the resort, I suppose?"

"Yes. There's a dance on tonight. St—someone's coming to pick me up at eight fifteen. I hope you don't object?"

"Not in the least," he said with a half smile that was little more than a grimace. "Why should I? I'm not your fiancé. . . . I'm surprised you've already found yourself an admirer, however."

"Oh, we city girls are fast workers," she said brightly, her cheeks staining with colour at the mention of her nonexistent fiancé.

"I'm already aware of that," he said dryly and, turning away, moved toward the door. "I'd better make haste with my fishing. It's a pity you didn't let me know your plans. We'll have to get together more often in the future and . . . synchronise our movements." His glance roamed slowly over her as he spoke and she bit her lip, her eyes riveted to his chest, the memory of its warmth, its texture, coming back to her with a painful reality that made her stomach churn.

He disappeared and she collapsed on the chair, her fingers to her mouth. Working for him was certainly totally different from working for Sylvia. It was unlike anything she'd imagined, and she wondered how long she was going to last. Just now she was so confused she didn't know if she wanted to go or to stay.

She showered while he was away, washed her hair, blow-dried it and then brushed it till it shone. She was trim in jeans and blue singlet top when he came back.

The fish was delicious. It was coral trout, and Aidan cooked it gently in butter, and made a pretty and delectable salad to accompany it. Guy opened a bottle of white wine and congratulated her.

"You're a better cook than Diane. Your fiancé's a lucky man—in that respect, at any rate. This is a meal to savour, to linger over. It's a shame you have to hurry away."

Was he mocking her with those last few words? She had no idea, but she murmured her thanks conventionally.

When she'd made the coffee, she didn't join him in the sitting room, but washed the dishes and then vanished to her bedroom, where she changed into a drifty dress of pale-green cotton that left one of her shoulders bare. The storm hadn't lasted long, but it had left the air hot and steamy, and even with the ceiling fan going, it was quite a problem to deal with makeup. She used a minimum, concentrating on her eyes and adding a little lip gloss. She didn't feel terribly keen on the idea of dancing, nor did she like the idea of getting her shoes wet walking through the wild tropical garden. She slipped her feet into rubber-soled thongs and, carrying her gold sandals, went onto the back annex well before Steve arrived at eight fifteen.

It was a pleasant evening in spite of the heat. The dance band was good, and Steve proved to be an accomplished dancer and a lot of fun. A blond girl with long hair, large brown eyes and a voluptuous figure played the guitar and sang a couple of songs—one of them her own composition—while the members of the band were having a break. Aidan was surprised to learn from Steve that she was Vanda Hardy. She was a really talented singer with a very bright personality that made her popular with the guests, particularly the male ones—though Steve professed to have eyes for no one but Aidan.

They danced again, and then she asked him to take her home, explaining that although it wasn't terribly late, she had to work in the morning.

"What about meeting for a swim first thing in the morning before you start work?" he suggested as they strolled back along the dark path, his arm about her waist. "Do you think your boss would object if I turned up on the beach?"

"He might," Aidan said, knowing he most definitely would. "It's a private beach, you know, and I don't really have the right to invite anyone there. Mr. Desailley likes to have the place to himself and he doesn't welcome trespassers. It's a fact that once you make an exception for one person, the next thing you know everyone's turning up. Peace and quiet are very important to a writer," she concluded reasonably.

"He sounds like a horribly unsociable type to me," Steve commented. "How old is he?"

"I have no idea," Aidan said coolly. She guessed he must be in the mid-thirties, since he was a friend of Michael Hamilton's, but the very fact that he was as young as that made it embarrassing to discuss his age. Living with him in the bungalow as she was, she didn't relish the thought of having Steve view the situation with suspicion. Not that she thought he would, she assured herself without a great deal of conviction.

"Let's forget your boss anyhow," Steve said, his arm tightening about her waist. "If I can't come round to your beach, how about you coming around to mine?"

Aidan agreed promptly. She surely didn't have to consult Guy about what she did before breakfast!

Steve kissed her good-night before they reached the bungalow, and though he kissed her enthusiastically, she couldn't reciprocate. She liked him, but somehow kissing him meant nothing and she was glad when at last he let her go, apparently quite unaware of her own lack of response.

"I'll see you in the morning," he whispered, pressing her to him briefly before he left her.

There was a light in Guy's room, but she went to bed undisturbed.

She woke early in the morning, got into her bikini and a short terry robe and tripped off to the beach at the resort, where she put in a pleasant half hour with Steve and met some of the other guests as well. Before she went back to the bungalow she'd agreed that if she could get away that night, she'd join Steve on a launch trip to one of the islands, where there was to be a Polynesian banquet and dancing. The launch would be leaving the Breakaway jetty at seven o'clock.

For the rest of the day, Aidan worked hard. She scarcely saw Guy—they scarcely exchanged two words—and she didn't know what to make of it. He didn't tell her his plans for the day but, then, he was under no compulsion to do that, and she simply didn't have an opportunity to ask him if it would be all right for her to go out that night.

During the morning a girl came over from the lodge to clean the house, and when she left she took the soiled linen with her to be laundered at the lodge.

Guy took the boat out around three o'clock in the afternoon, and ridiculously, Aidan felt he might have asked her if she'd like to come with him. She hoped he would dine at the resort that night. Vanda had told her he ate there several times a week, and it would suit her if he were to do so tonight. But he told her nothing.

The rest of the afternoon went by and the boat didn't come back. Aidan couldn't keep her mind on her work; she made mistake after mistake and had to retype several pages, to her annoyance. It was the kind of thing that had never happened when she'd been working for Sylvia, and she explained it by the fact that she was on edge about her date for tonight.

When six o'clock came and Guy was still not back, Aidan took a shower and dressed in a tangerine tunic and matching evening pants. A wide, soft, gold belt and a rosette to clip back her hair at one side completed the outfit. Looking at herself searchingly in the mirror, she thought she looked good. Her washed-out tan had sparked up after her exposure to the sun, and her eyes looked bright and clear, the green predominating over the grey, thanks to the help of some subtle eyeshadow.

She was dressed and standing on the front verandah when Guy came back, dark-jawed, unshaven, moody, his white jeans dirty, his torso bare, his thick, curling hair in wild disarray. He'd made a good catch of fish, and as he came onto the verandah he stared at Aidan standing there in her finery.

"Going out again tonight? I can't think you're dressed up on my behalf." His voice was harsh and grating, and his glance roamed over her in a critical way. She had the feeling that she wasn't looking nearly as good as she'd imagined.

She licked her upper lip nervously. "I was going out. But I suppose you expect me to stay in and cook your fish for you."

"Not necessarily." His lip curled and there was a restless, almost feverish, look about him that had her wondering if he was having problems with his book. Unexpectedly she felt a surge of sympathy for him. She knew how problems with work had affected Sylvia, how quickly her self-confidence had gone down the drain.

"I'm quite capable of feeding myself," he went on. "But I'm beginning to wonder how much more you're planning to whittle down the time you spend working for me. You're out morning, noon and night, aren't you? I don't know why I put up with you."

"You don't have to put up with me," she said after a frozen moment. "I'm here only for a trial period."

"So you are," he agreed, his smile cold. He pushed past her on his way inside. "I'll make a guess. Your boyfriend spends too much time working, and you came here for a good time. Am I right?"

"A good time?" she burst out. He smelt of the sea and she also could smell the fish he was carrying as she followed him through the house. "I'd hardly call it a good time to sit sweating over a typewriter half the day and spend the rest of it washing dishes and worrying about cooking dinner. Surely I can have a little time for recreation. Or do you expect me to be at your command every moment you're awake?"

He threw the fish on the kitchen table then turned to look at her, his hands on his hips, his eyes glittering angrily. "When I expect that of you, you can begin to complain. I'm not aware that I've interfered with your freedom so far, and I won't tonight. Go on. Buzz off. I don't need you around. I can do without your yapping in my ear. All I ask is a bit of peace and quiet, and that's one thing I don't seem able to have when you're on the rampage. I'm here to work, even if you're not."

"Well, bully for you," she said furiously, half under her breath. But of course he heard her and before she knew what was in his mind, he'd stepped round the table and gripped her by the shoulders, shaking her.

"You're an infernally cheeky girl, Miss Elliot. You

don't know the first thing about being a private secretary. All you think about is yourself and your own wants. I guess your aunt let you do exactly as you pleased and you expect the same of me. Well, you're a pretty girl, but that's not enough to persuade me to be indulgent. I know your kind only too well." His eyes bored into hers as he spoke and she felt herself tremble and go weak at the knees. Wildly, she thought he was going to crush her to him, to kiss her as he had kissed her two nights ago. . . .

She tore her eyes away from his, afraid of what he might read there.

"Let me go. I . . . I hate having you touch me," she said breathlessly, and he let her go instantly, his mouth and eyes hardening.

She was shaking as she ran to her room to fetch her evening purse and her shawl. As she hurried along the path through the dark garden, she knew she was making a complete failure of all she'd set out to do in accepting this position. She wasn't proving herself to be the perfect secretary by any means, and just now she wished quite passionately that she hadn't become so involved with Steve Guerney. She wasn't the least bit in love with him. The only thing was that he enabled her to get away from the bungalow, and perhaps to prove to Guy that she had no interest in him romantically. That his torrid lovemaking on the beach hadn't meant a thing to her . . .

She only just made it to the jetty before the launch, loaded with tourists, pulled out. Steve was waiting for her, and they leaped onto the boat together, laughing.

It should have been a fantastic night, and yet it wasn't. Aidan kept thinking of Guy, moody and alone at the bungalow. And when at a very late hour Steve saw her home, she didn't make another date with him but merely promised she'd see him on the beach one morning.

Vanda Hardy arrived at the bungalow the next morning.

Aidan, who had been working away at her typing and feeling very washed out as a result of her late night combined with the heat, had just made a pot of tea. Hearing someone knock on the door, she hurried through the house, anxious not to have Guy disturbed and to let herself in for trouble. Vanda stood on the verandah, her blond hair loose on her shoulders, white shorts and a closely fitting pink cotton vest showing off her smoothly tanned and shapely limbs. Her brown eyes made a quick check of Aidan as she smiled and told her, "I'm Vanda Hardy. We talked on the telephone the other day, remember? Where's Guy?"

"He's working," Aidan said quickly. "Would you like to come in and have a cup of tea? I've just made some this minute."

"Great," Vanda said instantly. She moved along the verandah to sit down in one of the cane chairs. "I won't stay long. Mustn't keep you from your work."

"I was just taking a break," Aidan said, and Vanda nodded sympathetically. "You look as if you really need it, you poor thing. You're not acclimatising too well, probably."

Aidan thought she was acclimatising perfectly well, but she merely said politely, "I'll fetch the tea. I shan't be a minute."

"I thought you might have come over to make my acquaintance before this," Vanda remarked when Aidan came back with the tray of tea things. "You're too young to be satisfied to keep your head down all day and every day and not have any fun or meet anyone. Is Guy really keeping you all that busy?"

"Busy enough," Aidan said. She handed Vanda a cup of tea and offered her the sugar. "But I have been over to the resort, as a matter of fact. I heard you singing the other evening, but it didn't seem an appropriate occasion to introduce myself to you."

Vanda looked at her sharply over her tea cup. In the daylight, Vanda didn't look as young as she had in the artificial light, and Aidan thought she used too much makeup.

"You weren't there with Guy, were you?"

"Oh, heavens, no." Aidan coloured slightly. "One of the guests invited me over. Steve Guerney. Do you know him?"

The other girl shrugged. "I can't say that I do. But I'm glad you're making an effort to mix around a bit. The danger in staying cooped up with one person is that you're likely to grow possessive, and imagine you're in love with him."

Aidan felt coldness rise in her.

"Are you talking about Guy Desailley?" she asked lightly, and Vanda looked at her sceptically.

"Of course I am. And don't tell me you're not susceptible to his charms. I've yet to meet a woman who isn't. Your predecessor certainly was."

"Diane?"

"Who else? How much has he told you about her?"

"Not much," Aidan said. She added, a little coolly, "We haven't spent much time gossiping. He merely explained that she went back to England because her mother is ill."

Vanda smiled cynically. "Maybe that's the way he chooses to see it. Men are notoriously slow when it comes to picking up emotional vibrations." She lowered her voice. "I can tell you why Diane left. She's had Guy all to herself for three years, and she just couldn't take it when she discovered he was seriously interested in another woman."

Aidan's heart performed some unexpected acrobatics. She'd had no idea Guy was seriously interested in another woman, and her surprise was plain in her face.

"I can see you didn't know." Vanda's brown eyes were a little malicious. "Guy and I have been friends for a very long time, but I was madly wrapped up in my singing career in the days before he took off for Europe. Now that he's back, we've more or less taken up from where we left off. Diane did everything she could think of to try to keep us apart, but when he simply stopped letting her come with him to the lodge when he was having dinner with me, I guess she realised it was the end. Frankly, I don't think her mother's all that ill. She simply saw the writing on the wall—or Guy drew her attention to it—and she made it an excuse to disappear without losing her dignity completely." She paused to pour herself some more tea and then changed the subject. "What made you take on this job, Aidan? I hope it wasn't hero worship or something like that. There's no percentage in it for you personally, I warn you."

"Don't worry. I don't intend falling in love with Guy," Aidan said calmly, though for some reason her heart was thumping. "I accepted this position because it's the kind of work I'm used to doing and for no other reason." Then she too changed the subject. "You mentioned your singing career. Is it because of that you're living on this island?"

"Good lord, no! This is only temporary. I've lived in Brisbane for years. I was teaching music and taking singing lessons when Guy went away; then I got into cabaret, and early this year I had my own television show. Just an hour once a week, but it was terrifically exciting. However, I contracted glandular fever three months ago, and after I left hospital I came home. I'm pretty well over my convalescence now, and I've been helping around the resort and singing a couple of nights a week, more or less to keep my hand in."

"You'll go back to Brisbane later on, will you?" Aidan asked cautiously as she too poured herself a second cup of tea.

"What a question!" Vanda said with a laugh. "I can't quite see Guy settling in Brisbane, can you? It's not cosmopolitan enough for him. Anyhow, all that's yet to be decided." She got to her feet. "You have to go back to your typewriter, I suppose. Don't bother about me. I know my way around, and I'm going to pop in and see Guy for a moment. There's a book he promised to lend me when we were talking the other night. I said I'd come over to pick it up."

Aidan frowned, feeling herself in something of a quandary. Guy hadn't left her any special instructions regarding Vanda. Was she, in whom apparently he had a deep interest, to be classed as an intruder, or was she not? She said cautiously, "Perhaps I could find the book without disturbing Guy, Vanda. What's the title?"

Vanda's brown eyes had gone hard. "I forget the exact title. But don't try to push me around, Aidan. You're behaving exactly like Diane. I want to see Guy. Isn't that plain enough?"

It wasn't plain enough, really. What was troubling Aidan was whether Guy would want to see Vanda right now.

"Guy's working, Vanda, " she said after a moment. She got up from her chair, wondering wildly if she should block the doorway. "He really doesn't like to be disturbed."

"Don't start playing the dragon with me," Vanda said, her voice cold. "I have special privileges where

Guy's concerned. I'm not going to break up his day's work, I'm only going to take a couple of minutes of his time. He's expecting me."

Aidan doubted that. She said firmly, "I'd better check with him first."

Vanda laughed aloud. "How absurd can you get! Why should it be better for you to disturb him than for me? If he's going to be annoyed, then I'll hear the brunt of it. It's nothing to do with you. Oh—and one more thing—I was going to invite you to come over to the lodge this evening at five thirty or so to have a drink. I'll ask Guy if he can spare you, shall I?" she finished with a little smile.

Aidan shrugged helplessly, and with another flashing smile Vanda tripped off. When Aidan took the tea tray through to the kitchen a couple of minutes later she could hear voices through Guy's half-open door. So apparently he didn't mind Vanda disturbing his work. Aidan should have been thankful, but instead she was angry. To think he'd never breathed a word about this romance between them! She went cold all over as she thought of that night on the beach. What would Vanda think if she knew he'd come home from an evening with her to indulge in a passionate scene with his secretary? It seemed a curious way for him to have behaved under the circumstances. She'd have thought he'd already satisfied his desire for . . .

She cut off her thoughts abruptly.

Back in her office she found it hard to concentrate on what she was doing, and her typing seemed to have gone completely haywire. She ripped out the page she was working on and tore it up. Then, instead of starting again, she sat in front of her typewriter thinking about the other girl and what she had said about herself and Guy. It wasn't unreasonable to think she would be the sort of girl who would appeal to Guy. She was attractive, lively, and very talented. And being closer to thirty than twenty would make her a suitable companion for a man of Guy's age. Probably he intended to marry now that he'd come back to Australia, and Vanda was most likely the reason why he was spending so much time on Breakaway Island. When he went to Sydney to look for a house, he'd probably take Vanda with him.

A sound made Aidan glance round. Vanda stood in the doorway, her cheeks flushed.

"I'm going now. It's okay for you to come over this evening, Aidan. I got my book," she added, holding it up briefly for Aidan's inspection. "I'll see you later."

She was gone, and Aidan tried once more to concentrate on her work. But she was not left in peace for long. A few minutes later, Guy stood where Vanda had been, glaring across the room at her.

"I thought I told you it was part of your work to keep intruders from disturbing my privacy," he said, his voice as cold as steel.

Aidan widened her eyes and swallowed hard. "I . . . I didn't think you'd regard Vanda Hardy as an intruder."

"I regard anyone as an intruder, including you. My morning's work's been ruined, thanks to you."

"Thanks to me? You didn't have to see her." Aidan flashed. "You could have told her you were busy instead of inviting her into your room and talking for half an hour."

His nostrils whitened. "It's your job to tell people I'm working. The damage was done the moment she came in the door and started talking."

"Then why don't you make sure she knows she can't interrupt you when you're working?"

"Don't try to pass the buck. You sent her in. Why didn't you find that damned book yourself? Was it too much trouble? Do you think *your* work is more important than mine?" Their eyes met, his hard and accusing, and she felt her cheeks go crimson with anger. It was Vanda who had insisted on seeing Guy, but it would be no good pushing that point, she thought, staring back at him unwaveringly. "And what was the idea insisting that she ask me if you could go over to the resort this evening? Do you think I care that much? You've never bothered about getting my permission before."

Aidan's face was pale now, and she stared at him speechlessly. She realised she'd made a very bad mistake in letting Vanda into the bungalow. Even if Guy were in love with the girl—and she was beginning to doubt that—he evidently believed in keeping his personal life and his working life in separate compartments. He was, in fact, as hard as he looked, she reflected, and yet he'd told her the other night that where women were concerned he had a soft heart!

She said tensely, "I'm sorry. It won't happen again. I just accepted that Vanda was a personal friend, and I didn't like to be so overbearing as to tell her she couldn't see you when she . . . she so obviously wanted to."

"Then in future just forget you want to be liked and assert yourself on my behalf. You can get me some lunch. I can't work now."

Aidan rose obediently and found that her limbs were shaking. He was waiting for her to go out of the room, but she stopped within three feet of him.

"I won't go out this evening if you don't want me to. It . . . it's unimportant."

His smile was hard. "It's unimportant to me too, I assure you." He snapped his fingers. "I don't care what you do in your free time."

She felt another flash of anger. "Maybe you don't, Mr. Desailley, but exactly when *is* my time free? I had an idea one of the drawbacks of this job was that I was expected to be available at all hours of the day and night."

"You're quite right. I didn't know *you* realised it, though, judging from your recent activities. But go ahead with your plans for this evening. And don't worry about coming back to dinner. I've had about all I can stand of argument and niggling."

"Thank you," she said sarcastically. Hatred for him welled up in her and somehow she was thankful for it. She stalked past him without another glance in his direction.

Chapter Five

He didn't go back to work after lunch. Instead, he went out in the boat, and Aidan went back to her typewriter, noting that there was another stack of papers on her desk.

She was feeling ragged by the time she reached the resort at a little after five. Guy hadn't come back, and she was all nerves; she could hardly keep her mind off him. It disturbed her that she was making such a hash of working for him. She knew it was largely her own fault. She knew she should be agreeable and do her best to please him, at least with regard to her duties, and yet she was continually arguing with him, making scenes, slipping up on the things he expected of her, like guarding his peace. It seemed to her that it must be only a matter of time before he dismissed her. But meanwhile, there was that backlog of work he wanted done, and since she was efficient enough in that quarter, she supposed he'd tolerate her a little longer. But the relationship was becoming decidedly strained.

She had no idea where she was supposed to meet Vanda, so she went to Reception, where a middle-aged woman with dark-auburn hair asked pleasantly what she could do for Aidan.

"Could you tell me where to find Vanda Hardy? She's expecting me. I'm Aidan Elliot," she added.

The expression on the other woman's face changed instantly, the pleasant friendliness disappearing like magic. She gave Aidan a thorough scanning, taking in her soft white cotton pants and sleeveless green top, her shining brown hair caught back behind one ear and looped up with a white band for coolness.

"So you're the girl who's working for Mr. Desailley," she said finally. "I'm Louise Hardy, by the way. My husband told me he thought it was irresponsible of your people to allow you to come and work here, and I can see what he meant. A young girl like you!" She pursed her lips disapprovingly. "You may not like it, but I'm going to give you some advice."

Aidan felt herself bristle with antagonism at the woman's tone.

"So what *is* your advice, Mrs. Hardy?" she asked, her voice cool.

"To tell Guy Desailley you'd prefer to sleep over here at the lodge, and to insist he arranges it," Louise Hardy said crisply. "You can imagine what people must think when they know you're over there alone with him day and night."

Aidan's eyes flashed with anger. "People?" she repeated. "So far as I know, there's practically no one at this resort who even knows I exist. But perhaps you mean yourself."

"Perhaps I do," the other woman said, a quick flush rising from her neck into her face. "I certainly wouldn't allow a daughter of mine to live with a man the way you're doing."

"I'm not living with a man, Mrs. Hardy." Aidan forced herself to speak quietly. "I'm working for Mr. Desailley. Our relationship is purely a business one, and if it were not, merely sleeping somewhere else at night wouldn't make any difference."

Louise's glance sharpened. "It's easy to talk, Miss Elliot. But mark my words, you're storing up trouble for yourself. Guy Desailley is an attractive man, and in no time you'll be getting ideas about him. Don't expect any sympathy from me if you finish up with no job and a broken heart. He'd never marry you, you know."

"I don't happen to want him to marry me," Aidan said brusquely. She felt like turning on her heel and walking out, but before she did so she repeated her first request. "Do you know where I'll find Vanda?"

"In the bar, or down at the poolside, most likely," Louise Hardy said curtly. "I can't be expected to know her every movement. You'll have to look around for yourself."

"Thank you." Aidan turned away and walked quickly outside.

She found Vanda by the pool talking to a group of young people. When she saw Aidan, Vanda excused herself and came to greet her.

"Hello! So you came. Let's go inside to the bar. You look absolutely boiling."

I am—with rage, Aidan thought, but she didn't say it aloud. The bar was cooled by ceiling fans, and Vanda asked for two glasses of punch and took Aidan to a secluded area where some cane chairs, made comfortable with cushions, were arranged around a low table with a glass top.

"I can't spend much time with you," she remarked, looking Aidan over in much the same way that her mother had. "I'm singing a bracket of numbers tonight and I want to practise them. What are you planning to do with yourself? If you feel like having a meal in the restaurant, I'll see that you're put at a table with some people around your own age."

"Don't bother. I think I'd better go back to the bungalow," Aidan said after a second. "Guy went out in the boat this afternoon, but I expect he'll want dinner when he comes back."

Vanda sent her a scathing look. "You're his secretary, not his wife," she said. "And if you want to hang on to your job, take my advice and don't cling to him like a limpet. That's one reason I asked you over this evening, as a matter of fact—to encourage you to spread your interests. Diane didn't, and it was really pathetic. She used to come over here with him and then just sit gazing at him. It's a wonder he didn't tell her off in front of everyone. She acted like a lovesick girl of eighteen, though she was close to forty and big as well. Oh, she was attractive enough in a mature kind of way, but not the sort of woman Guy fancies at all."

It occurred to Aidan from the way Vanda was talking on and on about Diane that she had some kind of a complex about her, and as Vanda paused to raise her glass to her lips, Aidan seized the opportunity to remark, "Well, you can forget about Diane now, can't you? She's safely out of the way in England and unlikely to come back."

Vanda's brown eyes looking at her over the glass were hard. "I'm telling you this for your own good, Aidan. Because as I remarked this morning when you tried to stop me from seeing Guy—to stop *me!*—you're beginning to act exactly like Diane. I was polite to her, but I'm not going to be quite so polite to you. If you try to come between me and Guy again, I'll make very sure you're off this island and out of work in double-quick time. Do you understand?"

Aidan discovered she was trembling. Was this why Vanda had asked her to come here this evening? To say the things she hadn't dared to say at Guy's bungalow? She set her glass down and got to her feet.

"Now you've got that off your mind, I think I'd better leave, Vanda. Thank you for the drink—and the warning, which I assure you is quite unnecessary. I haven't the slightest intention of trying to break up whatever's between you and Guy." She should have stopped there, but she didn't. "In the future I'd be glad if you'd mind your own business and leave me to manage mine. It's up to Guy to decide what my duties are, and one of them is to see that he's not disturbed, so it's no use threatening me. If you don't like it, you'll have to talk to Guy about it."

Vanda jumped to her feet, her eyes blazing. "Who do you think you are, talking to me like that? My parents are running this resort and you have the cheek to come here and act as if you own the place."

Aidan looked back at her coldly, hoping her inner turmoil didn't show.

"You invited me here, Vanda. Perhaps you'd rather I kept away in future?"

Vanda gave an exclamation of anger and walked away.

Aidan sat down again. She was shaking. She wished she'd held her tongue, but it seemed to be a habit of hers to say more than she meant to. She didn't know what she was going to do now. The thought of going back to the bungalow right away didn't attract her, yet what else was there to do? She couldn't sit around here on her own for the rest of the afternoon.

Her problem was solved a minute later when Steve

walked into the bar, saw her and came toward her, smiling.

"Aidan! You're just the person I wanted to see. What are you doing here? You haven't got a date with somebody else, have you?"

"No." She managed a smile, and to tell the truth, it was cheering to have someone as normal and friendly as Steve appear at this moment. "I'm all by myself. Are you going to join me?"

"I sure am—when I've got myself a drink and another one for you. Punch?"

"Yes, please." She watched him go across to the bar, young and husky and healthy-looking in white shorts and shirt. It would be nice to fall in love with someone as uncomplicated as that, she reflected, and then caught herself up on the thought. Anyone would think she'd fallen in love with someone who wasn't uncomplicated, but the fact was, she wasn't in love with anyone. Or so she assured herself.

Steve came back with the drinks and sat down opposite her. "I've been playing tennis. I was thinking of walking over to the bungalow to see if you were about. I've only another week left here, you know. How about staying and having dinner with me tonight? We can dance afterward. You look like a million dollars in that outfit."

"Flatterer," she said with a laugh, but it was nice to have him look at her that way, as if he really liked her. So many people lately seemed to have been looking at her as if she were their least favourite person. "I suppose I could stay—though I might get into trouble about it afterward." In fact, she surely would, she thought ruefully, but at the moment she felt reckless.

"Fantastic!" Steve said. "Listen—suppose we take our drinks outside to the pool. You can sit there and watch what's going on while I shower and change. Only mind you keep your eyes off any other young and virile males! I promise you I'll be back in a flash."

"Right," Aidan agreed, smiling again and determining to put Vanda and Louise Hardy and Guy, too, right out of her mind, and simply enjoy herself. She had a feeling her days on Breakaway Island were coming to an end fairly soon in any case, and tomorrow—tomorrow she'd make up for any time she'd wasted today. She'd astound Guy with the amount of work she'd get through and she'd keep her head down and be really conscientious.

Steve left her under an umbrella, leaning back in a lounger, her drink close by. She stared at the glittering blue water of the pool, and the people enjoying themselves there, and wished she'd brought her bikini with her. If she were staying here instead of at the bungalow, as Louise Hardy had said she should, she'd probably have a great time. But she was here to work, not to have a holiday, and Guy had told her right from the start that being on the spot was part of the job. Of course she wasn't always on the spot, she reflected uneasily. She was even planning to stay at the resort for the next few hours, whether he wanted her or not. She was beginning to understand why he'd said she wasn't at all the sort of secretary he wanted. Diane had been about forty, according to Vanda, and he must have expected that Michael would send him someone about the same age.

Instead, *she'd* turned up and caused friction between them right from the start by opening her mouth too wide.

Someone sat down on the end of the next lounger, and Aidan turned her head in surprise, thinking Steve had been impossibly quick. But it wasn't Steve. It was Guy, and her heart gave a little leap in her breast. He was immaculate in a cream shirt and closely fitting dark pants, his usually rumpled hair was combed, his jaw was newly shaved and he looked stunningly handsome. Aidan sat up slowly, her eyes fixed on him as though he were an apparition.

"What are you doing here?" she demanded.

He smiled wryly, his teeth white against the tan of his skin. "Surely I have as much right to be here as you have," he said in a voice that did something quite drastic to her metabolism, it was so unusually soft and almost wooing.

She coloured slowly and deeply.

"I'm sorry. I . . . I'd been wondering if I should go back to the bungalow . . . if . . . if you wanted me to cook a meal. . . ."

"Muhammad has come to the mountain," he said, his eyes moving to her mouth in a way that sent a shiver all through her. "I thought, since you were presumably having a pre-dinner drink with Vanda, you might then have dinner with me in the restaurant here."

Aidan swallowed, her throat dry, her pulse racing. She must be hearing things. He'd surely never in a fit ask her to have dinner with him. Besides, what would Vanda think? She discovered her eyes were locked with his, and her lips parted softly; then just as she was about to accept his invitation—because how could she possibly, possibly refuse it, she thought confusedly— she remembered. She was having dinner with Steve. It was like a dash of icy water bringing her back to reality.

"I . . . I'd love to, but I'm afraid I can't," she said in dismay.

His dark eyes grew darker. "Can't? What do you mean? Haven't you just said you were wondering if you should be going back to the bungalow?"

Oh, what a fool she was making of herself! She bit her lip in confusion. "I forgot. I . . . I more or less promised . . . I told Steve I'd have dinner with him if I could," she stammered, and saw his eyes harden and grow cold.

"I'm beginning to wonder just how involved you are with Steve," he said curtly. "For a girl who's engaged, you certainly go out of your way to seek the company of other men. But perhaps Robert shares your ideas of independence and freedom."

"Perhaps he does," she retorted. "And anyhow— why should it be all right for me to have dinner with you and not with Steve?"

He smiled in a way that was somehow savage. "Because my motives in asking you are undoubtedly very different from his."

She wanted to protest, to ask him what he meant, but she decided the less said, the better. He'd turned his head to look at the swimmers in the pool, and it occurred to her that he was possibly wondering which of them was Steve.

"He's not there," she said. "He's gone to change." Her eyes went back to Guy and he looked back at her coldly.

"Whom did you meet here, Aidan? Vanda, or your new heartthrob?"

"Vanda, of course," she exclaimed hotly. "You know that perfectly well. She asked you if it would be all right."

He shrugged. "You put her up to that. . . . Would you like another drink? I'm going to get myself a whisky."

"Go ahead," she said coolly. "Don't worry about me. I'm quite happy to wait here for Steve."

Without another word he got up and left her, and she watched him go, aware of a feeling of frustration and disappointment, and not caring at this moment to investigate the exact cause of it.

She didn't see him again until she was in the restaurant. He was there already when she went in with Steve and to her dismay the waitress, a pretty dark-haired girl in a sarong, took them to a table and seated her so that she was facing him. There was no way she could alter the arrangement without making embarrassing explanations, so she gave in to the inevitable. At least he was halfway across the room. He was on his own, and during the meal she caught his eye so many times it was almost as if they were together. Except, of course, that there was no spoken communication between them.

When dinner was over and Steve suggested that they go into the lounge and dance, she agreed eagerly.

Guy was still sitting alone at his table as they left the restaurant, and deliberately she didn't look at him, and equally deliberately she tried to put him out of her mind. She found it remarkably difficult. It was absurd that she should keep thinking of him, and she remembered uneasily what Vanda had said about Diane sitting gazing at him. But quite positively she, Aidan, hadn't done that. It was certainly strange too, that every time she had looked at him, he had been looking back at her. . . .

While she and Steve were dancing, Vanda came to the microphone and sang. She had an undeniably attractive voice, slightly husky and very sexy, and she knew how to move her body and her hands. She was tremendously popular with everyone in the big room, including Steve. She was halfway through her second song when Guy came through the double doors. Aidan, by some curious chance, saw him at once. He stood leaning nonchalantly against the wall, smoking a cigarette—which he never did inside his own bungalow —and looking at Vanda. Vanda too was instantly aware of him, and it seemed to Aidan that she put an extra throb in her voice as she looked toward him and directed the romantic words of her song to him.

Well, why wouldn't she, when there was a close relationship between them? Or so she said, though Aidan still found it hard to accept.

Aidan turned away from him deliberately and gave all her attention to Steve.

"It's too hot for dancing," he murmured presently. "Why don't we go outside for a while and take a walk along the beach?"

"Sounds like a good idea." Aidan acquiesced, all too willing to get away from the sight of Guy transfixed by Vanda and her songs. Steve put his arm around her waist, and as they left the dance floor, Aidan's eyes met Guy's briefly and she felt such a shock go through her that she had to cling to Steve's arm to prevent her knees from giving way. What on earth was happening to her? she wondered dazedly.

On the beach, Steve kissed her quite passionately. She'd known he intended doing that, but she couldn't respond. She'd been in his arms for only a couple of minutes when she pulled away and suggested tentatively, "Let's go back and have one more dance, Steve. And then I really must go home."

He agreed after only a slight protest.

In the lounge, Guy was still there. He sat by himself, a glass of Scotch in his hand. Vanda was singing again, yet it was at Aidan Guy looked as she and Steve came in, went onto the floor, and began to dance.

When the dance was over, Steve found a seat for her and told her, "I'll get you a drink. What would you like?"

"Oh, a fruit drink of some kind," she said nervously. "Nothing alcoholic."

She wasn't surprised, somehow, to find Guy coming toward her once Steve had vanished in the direction of the bar.

"So that's the man who's menacing your engagement, is it?" he said, leaning over the back of her chair so she could feel the warmth of his breath, his lips, against the back of her neck.

She didn't answer but she felt herself shiver inwardly and she closed her eyes briefly.

"What do you see in him, Aidan?"

The reaction his nearness drew from her was intolerable, and she drew away from him, smelling the whisky on his breath.

"I wish you'd stop breathing down my neck. You . . . you've been drinking. Leave me alone."

"I've had a couple of whiskies," he said, his voice slightly thick. "Do you call that drinking? And why don't you answer my question? What do you want from other men? Aren't you satisfied with the one you have back in Sydney—the one you've promised to marry?"

Her cheeks flamed. "It's none of your business, Mr. Desailley."

"Mr. Desailley," he mocked, and now his lips were caressing her neck. "Well, let's assume I'm keeping an eye on you on Robert's behalf—and hoping to persuade you to behave yourself and come home."

"Steve will see me home," she said stiffly.

"He needn't bother, Miss Elliot. I happen to be going your way."

She gritted her teeth. She could see Steve coming toward her, carrying two glasses of fruit juice, but there was absolutely nothing she could do about the man who was leaning over the back of her chair, his lips moving lightly over her neck and disturbing her unbearably.

Before Steve could say anything, she sat forward jerkily, and introduced the two men. Guy had straightened up to stand beside her chair almost possessively, and Aidan felt highly embarrassed, the more so because she was aware that he was not altogether sober. She knew it was a shock to Steve to find her employer so young and personable. He'd probably pictured him a whole lot older and not nearly so handsome, though there was an aggressive look about Guy just now that was far from attractive, and was due, Aidan was sure, to the fact that he'd been drinking. Not two whiskies as he'd said, but more than he could take without losing at least a little of his usual self-control.

The two men sat down, Guy apparently taking it for granted that he was welcome to join them, and Aidan drank her lemon squash and tried to think of something matter-of-fact to say. It was beyond her comprehension that Guy should be inflicting himself on her and Steve, and she could only guess what thoughts must be going through Steve's mind at the realisation that she was living alone in a bungalow with such a man.

It was actually a relief when Vanda, her bracket of songs finished, came to make a foursome, sitting next to Guy and remarking rather pointedly, "That's my last number for tonight. Now I can relax. I'd just love a drink."

"I'm sure Steve will look after your needs, Vanda," Guy said, one eyebrow tilting rakishly. "Aidan and I must be making tracks. We have a working day ahead of us tomorrow."

Vanda glared at Aidan as if she'd like to kill her, and Steve went red in the face. Aidan was furious with Guy for interfering so high-handedly in her personal life, but there was nothing she could do without creating a scene.

"Sorry, Steve," she said after a moment. "I don't want to go, but it looks as if I must. It's been a lovely evening, anyhow."

Guy got to his feet lazily and held out a hand to her, but she ignored it and went over to Steve, and looked at him ruefully. "You understand, don't you? I'd love to stay—to dance again. But I really do have to get up early in the morning. And there's no point in your walking all the way to the bungalow and back."

"Okay, if that's how you want it." He spoke far from graciously, and she clenched her fists.

"It's not, but . . ."

Vanda gave a muffled exclamation and jumped to her feet.

"I've changed my mind about wanting a drink. Besides, there's something I have to see to." Her eyes were fixed on Guy, but in response he merely smiled and wished her a brisk good-night. With a poisonous look at Aidan, she walked rapidly away.

Guy took Aidan's arm. She felt a shiver run along her nerves at his touch before she brushed his fingers off and told Steve quickly, "I'll see you in the morning on the beach, Steve."

His smile was decidedly cool, but he murmured, "Oh, sure. Good-night, Aidan." Deliberately he leaned forward and kissed her on the mouth; then without bothering to say good-night to Guy, he strode off across the room as though he too had something urgent to attend to.

Chapter Six

Outside, Aidan kept her distance from Guy as they made their way along the gravel path to the gate. Quite positively she wasn't going to put up with this kind of interference in her life without uttering a protest, but she said nothing as they walked along the dark, shadowy path through the wild tropical garden, their footsteps silent. Now and again Guy shone his flashlight ahead and then flicked it off again, and somehow Aidan's anger began to simmer down. She found she was becoming so electrifyingly conscious of the man at her side that it became almost impossible for her to concentrate her thoughts on Steve, and her own annoyance at what had just happened at the resort.

But presently, drawing a deep breath, she forced herself to tell Guy coldly, "I don't care for the way you behaved just now."

"Oh? What did I do to offend you?" he asked in mock surprise.

"As if you didn't know!" she exclaimed. "You took

over, you acted as if . . . as if you owned me body and soul."

She heard his low laugh. "You're romanticising, Miss Elliot. If I felt that way about you, I wouldn't have been so damned polite to that young man you're amusing yourself with. I'd have punched him on the nose."

"What on earth are you talking about?" she gasped, feeling a shock run along her nerves. "I wasn't implying you . . . you . . . I only meant . . ."

She broke off, confused, and he said cynically, "I know exactly what you meant, Aidan. You've convinced yourself I gave your friend the impression that our relationship is far from a purely business one."

"So what sort of impression do *you* think you gave him?" she demanded, annoyed by his insistence that she was romanticising.

"I have no idea and I don't care in the least. Do *you* care all that much? Is he so important in your life—a man you've only met two or three times?"

"I don't have to discuss my private life with you," she retorted. "And that's exactly what I object to—your . . . your interference in my personal life. But perhaps you don't allow your secretaries to have a personal life, Mr. Desailley."

"It would make life a whole lot easier for me if they didn't," he said with wry humour. "However, it's not mandatory." As he spoke, he took her arm in such a casual way she couldn't bring herself to pull away from him. "But let's not go on with this pointless argument, Aidan. Look at it this way. I've thrown my weight around to get you home at a reasonable hour, and that's all there is to it. You're no use to me if you stay out half the night and haven't got your wits about you the next day."

"Oh, your work! That's all you ever think about,

isn't it," she snapped, feeling somehow cut down to size.

"That's the way I like it," he said tersely. "But right at this moment, my work couldn't be further from my mind."

Aidan's heart gave a little thud. "What . . . what do you mean?" She heard him mutter something under his breath and then he let go of her arm.

"Walk ahead of me. The path gets narrow here. Take the flashlight." He thrust it into her hand and she took it with fingers that trembled.

She was quite sure he'd been on the brink of saying something quite different. But no doubt she was romanticising again, she thought in frustration. She flashed the flashlight ahead of her briefly and walked on. The air was soft and warm and filled with the scent of flowers, and through the faint clatter of the palm leaves in the night wind, she seemed to hear the erratic beating of her own heart. Or was it his?

As if it were imperative to stop her imagination from getting out of hand, she said over her shoulder, "I've been meaning to ask you about this garden. It's not really wild, is it? Someone planted it—the shrubs, the trees, the flowers. Designed it all. Laid out the paths—built the little bridge."

"My parents," he said. He caught up with her and began to walk next to her once more. His arm brushed against hers now and again, and though she found his merest touch unnerving, she didn't move away. "They lived here for several years after my mother contracted a terminal illness. Earlier, when I was still at school, we used to holiday here, and I'd swim and fish and explore all day long and half the night, while they were happy with each other's company. Probably my roots as a novelist were put down at that time. I'd just gone into journalism when my parents moved here permanently.

They'd already established a small resort on the island, but they lived alone in the bungalow and laboured together to create this garden—their temporary Eden." He stepped behind her to avoid an overhanging branch and then came level with her again.

"And your mother," Aidan said thoughtfully. "Did she die here?"

"They both died here—during a cyclone. I've often wondered whether . . ." He broke off. "But I'm talking too much. It must be all that whisky you accused me of drinking. I mustn't bore my secretary to tears after dragging her away from the fun she so obviously craves, must I?"

He spoke ironically, and Aidan exclaimed in annoyance, "You're not boring me. I'm interested. Were you implying just now that your parents—deliberately—lost their lives in the cyclone because of your mother's illness—and their love for each other?"

"Maybe I was. Though I didn't intend to communicate it to you, Aidan. That kind of love is probably incomprehensible to you. I doubt whether it exists these days. Self is what matters most—self-discovery, self-realisation, self-expression. Freedom. Liberation. Loyalty's out of fashion and so is trust. Love is a garden I'll certainly never venture into again. Its flowers have turned putrid—they stink."

"You sound so cynical!" she exclaimed, shocked by the harshness of his tone.

"I am cynical," he countered dryly. "I'm encouraged to be that way by what I see about me. Why are you marrying, for instance?"

She felt her cheeks flame in the darkness. She should have been able to answer, "For love," but of course she couldn't. "Why . . . why do you think?" she stammered instead.

"Well, let me see now," he drawled, reaching out to

put his arm around her shoulders and draw her against him casually. "I'll admit I'm only guessing, but I imagine it's for purely practical reasons. I don't imagine it's for love. If it were, then you wouldn't be here now, would you?"

"Here?" she stammered, trying to pull away from him but being drawn back remorselessly. "What do you mean? I . . . I didn't ask you to see me home, Mr. Desailley, Or to . . . to put your arm around me . . ."

"Oh, for God's sake, don't be so literal," he exclaimed. "We're not talking about this minute. I mean you wouldn't be here on this island having fun. You're no more in love with Robert—or with Steve—than you are with me. You're just having a great time, aren't you? Flirting with all and sundry, running off to meet strangers, taking in all the kissing and whatever that comes your way."

"Kissing and whatever? Exactly what's that supposed to mean?" She choked on her words and almost blurted out that she wasn't in love with anyone, wasn't engaged to Robert, but what purpose would it serve to admit she'd lied to him? For all she knew, he might even take it as an invitation, though an invitation to what, she didn't explain to herself.

"This kind of thing," he said, and with a smooth and unexpected movement, he pulled her into his arms and held her close to him, his head bent, his breathing deep, his heart thumping against the softness of her breast. She hadn't a notion why she didn't resist, or why she let him hold her that way. Her common sense was telling her to remember the things he'd said, to run for the bungalow as fast as she could and shut herself in her room. But she didn't listen to her common sense. She didn't resist, she didn't run, and as she stood crushed against his maleness, feeling the heat of his body burning into her flesh, his breath mingling with her own, she knew she didn't want to be anywhere else but here. It was as though a door was slowly opening and she was waiting for something. The blood began to race wildly through her veins, sensations and emotions she'd never been aware of before stirred to life deep within her, and every inch of her became shatteringly aware of his body, his closeness, his maleness.

Slowly she raised her head to stare into the dark shadows that were his eyes. She no longer cared what he'd been saying. All she cared about was that they were here in the darkness together, Aidan Elliot and Guy Desailley, and he was holding her in his arms and they were both filled with desire—drawn inexorably together by the mere fact of their sexuality. Yet some part of her knew it was not as simple as that; that for her it had to be *this* man—that for her, Guy Desailley was unique.

A frightening feeling of excitement surged through her, and she breathed his name almost inaudibly. "Guy . . ."

There was a long pause. He didn't move, but merely looked down into her eyes.

"Kiss me," she whispered huskily.

His mouth came down on hers instantly and demandingly, and he strained her against him as if he couldn't get her close enough. She found herself responding to his hungry kisses as though she knew all there was to know about passion. Everything went out of her mind except the pleasure, the ecstasy, of this moment, with their bodies so close, their lips, warm and moist and searching, telling her things about herself, and about him, arousing sensations that were so exquisite, they were scarcely to be borne.

His mouth moved from hers for a moment so they could both breathe, and he shifted her slightly so her back was against the smooth, broad trunk of a tree.

Spangles of moonlight glittered in her eyes as his lips traced a trail from the corner of her mouth to her neck just under her ear, touching her skin sensitively, sending shivers of delight all through her body. Neither of them spoke but she could feel the warmth of his breath, hear the soft *click-clack* of the palm leaves, feel the rise and fall of her breast, as her breathing, quickened by passion, went out of control. She moved against him sensually, lifting her hand to seek the thick, curling hair at the back of his neck, to pull his head against her. His mouth was on the smooth, bare flesh of her shoulder, trailing its way down. Little pulses seemed to beat a tattoo all over her body. Her head tilted back, her eyes closed as his touch went to her breast, and the warmth of his lips continued to tantalise her.

At last he groaned and moved away from her; then he put his arm around her shoulders and pulled her to him roughly and said thickly, "We can't stand here making love all night. Let's start walking."

She didn't say anything—couldn't—and what he meant she could only guess. She had the half-frightened, half-excited feeling he was going to ask her to let him continue his lovemaking when they got back to the bungalow, and right at this moment she knew she didn't even want to say no. A voice inside her head was saying urgently, Why not? It has to happen. You've been waiting for this all your life. She felt completely helpless, completely under the spell of passion to which, until now, she'd been almost a complete stranger.

His arm was still about her and her legs were trembling when at last they reached the bungalow. There, he drew her inside, into the stifling warmth of the verandah, and holding her closely, he kissed her deeply and druggingly. When his lips left hers, her fingers clung to him and she pulled him back to her.

It was a distinct shock when he took her by the wrists and drew her hands down, and instead of asking her to come to bed with him, he said jerkily, "I'm going down to the beach to take a swim."

Before she'd really taken in the sense of what he was saying, he was on his way through the house.

After a moment she followed him as though she were bewitched, her footsteps taking her through the kitchen, along the hallway and onto the front verandah. She walked down the steps into the moonlit garden, hearing the soft sound of the sea, following Guy's shadow as it disappeared into the deeper shadow of the palms. Ahead of her he emerged onto the dazzling white sand, which was narrowed by the high tide, and she saw him strip off his clothes and stand for a moment, his body beautiful as sculptured marble, his muscles rippling, before he moved down to the water. She watched as he waded in, submerged himself and then began to swim away from her into the liquid silver of the sea.

Aidan wrapped her arms around her and shivered suddenly, although the air was heavy and humid and warm. Guy hadn't looked back and was probably quite unaware of her presence. After a moment, she too shed her clothes, scrambling out of them hastily before running down to the water. It was soft and warm and silky and she began to swim out toward the dark shadow on the silver sea that was Guy. It was fantastic swimming naked at night. The feeling of freedom was heavenly. Her body seemed to glide through the water as easily as a fish, and yet however fast she swam, she didn't get any nearer to Guy. His dark head turned toward her once, but perhaps he didn't see her, for he kept swimming, and always away from her.

Presently she abandoned her pursuit of him and floated on her back, revelling in the embrace of the water and staring up at the starry sky.

She was startled out of her dream by his voice, and discovered he was close enough to touch.

"I'm going in, Aidan. You'd better not stay out here on your own."

He swam away from her and she followed him, but without a hope of catching up.

He was already collecting his clothes as she waded through the shallows onto the sand, and she knew he was watching her as she moved towards her own little heap of clothing. She was tinglingly conscious of her small, firm breasts, her flat stomach, her long, slender legs, and she more than half expected him to come toward her—to touch her, to say her name, to take her in his arms.

But he didn't, and when she'd collected her clothes they moved through the palms together without speaking. Once his hand brushed against the back of her wrist and she felt a thrill like an electric current run up her nerves. Her body was drying rapidly, and as they reached the bungalow, the air became closer and more breathless.

On the verandah, Guy held the screen door open for her and as she walked past him he said in a quiet, aloof voice, "Good night, Aidan."

"Good night . . . Guy." She paused and glanced up at him, and then quickly looked away. His black eyes were so distant, so devoid of expression, that she was suddenly deeply and embarrassingly conscious of her nakedness. She hurried through the house away from him.

Her bedroom was hot. She switched on the fan and the bedside lamp and then went into the bathroom to take a shower and wash the salt from her body and her hair. Her face in the mirror was flushed, her eyes dark and passionate, and her lips trembled as if they were waiting to be kissed again. But she knew quite certainly that Guy wouldn't come to her room tonight, and to her shame, she knew too that she ached to have him come— to have him take her in his arms, to kiss her as he'd kissed her earlier. . . .

Her cheeks burning, she turned away from the mirror and stepped under the shower.

She woke early. It wasn't yet six o'clock, the sky through her window was a pale, pearly pink, and she lay quite still, listening for another sound through the birdcalls and the soft wash of the sea on the beach. Listening for sounds of Guy moving in the house, and not hearing them. She'd told Steve she'd join him for a swim before breakfast, but she was going to break her promise. She didn't want to see Steve or even to think of him. Her mind was full of Guy and the confused and confusing happenings of last night. Right now, she simply couldn't make sense of any of it, and she began to go over and over it in her mind. What had it all meant? Had their relationship changed as drastically as it seemed to her? Had Guy minded leaving her the way he had last night? Had he wanted to come to her room, to make love to her?

As she recalled their conversation just before he'd taken her in his arms, a faint shiver ran across her skin and she moved restlessly, clasping her hands behind her head and stretching her legs, naked under the fine cotton sheet. She'd asked him what he meant by saying she'd been letting other men kiss her and "whatever." And he'd explained "whatever" as being "this kind of thing." Which meant that for him, it had been completely calculated, completely meaningless.

Oh! That had gone right out of her mind in her own delight in his lovemaking. She'd even begged him to kiss her. And then she'd followed him into the sea. He hadn't invited her, and he hadn't meant her to come—

she was sure of it now. That was why she hadn't been able to catch up with him in the water. He hadn't wanted her there. She felt sick with shame as she remembered how she'd walked across the sand, wet from the sea and completely naked. What on earth must he think of her? Worse, still, he'd said earlier that he'd never fall in love again—never venture again into the garden of love. Romantic words spoken so cynically, they'd shocked her.

She turned her face into the pillow with a little muffled cry. She knew without doubt that she was in love with him—desperately, hopelessly, madly—though she'd known him less than a week. Thank goodness she'd told him she was going to marry another man. It would be unbearable if he knew how she felt about him.

She closed her eyes and discovered his image there, discovered she was imagining his body against her own—cool from the sea, his kisses tasting of salt. She could feel her fingers in his wet, curling black hair, see his dark eyes looking into hers in the starlight.

With a smothered sob, she got out of bed and groped for her clothes. If she had any sense, she'd go round to Breakaway Beach and meet Steve, but she couldn't—she couldn't. Even though she dreaded a face-to-face encounter with Guy, she longed for it as well. She had to know what his attitude toward her was going to be, and she was desperately afraid he'd tell her to pack her things and go back to Sydney. After all, she was here only on trial, and he'd told her very clearly that they were to keep sex out of their relationship. Yet he was the one who'd started it. And she'd encouraged him, she thought, furious with herself and wanting to weep as well.

She brushed her hair at the window, unable to face her own reflection. Some crazy voice in the depths of her mind was telling her impossible things—such as that despite himself, Guy had fallen in love with her, that he wouldn't let her go.

"Fool!" she told herself, and tossed down her brush.

Steeling herself, she left her room. The sooner she faced up to reality the better, no matter what sort of reality it turned out to be.

When she got to the kitchen she found he'd already breakfasted and was shut up in his study. That in itself was a frustration. Not to see him—even though she'd been dreading it. Not to be able to get any idea at all of how he felt about last night. Though perhaps his avoidance of her was an indication in itself. Yet *was* he avoiding her? she wondered wryly later as she started to work in her own small office. Maybe he wasn't even thinking of her. He was much worldlier and more sophisticated than she was. He'd probably put last night completely out of his mind with no trouble at all. Whereas she found it impossible to think of anything else.

At midday, a telephone call came through from Sydney—a personal call for Guy—and she went to his study to tell him.

"You're wanted on the telephone, Guy. I'm sorry, but it's Sydney—a personalised call, so I can't take it."

"Okay, I'll be right along."

His dark, curling hair was ruffled and his face was unsmiling as he left his desk and came toward her. Their eyes met for a single, searing instant, and then he brushed past her. Aidan, trembling at the mere sight of him, went out to the kitchen. She might as well prepare some lunch, she thought, and she knew she was hoping, now that his work had been interrupted, that he would eat with her and that they'd talk. About anything at all.

From the kitchen she could hear his voice quite clearly, and when she realised it was Michael Hamilton calling him, she listened deliberately, her heart beating fast.

"Oh, is that you, Michael? How are things? I believe you've been over in Perth." A long pause, and somehow she knew that Michael was talking about her, and she wondered uneasily if he were backing up Shay's choice of her as a secretary, but she soon discovered he was not. "Yes, you're quite right, and I won't pretend I was delighted when she turned up on the doorstep. She's efficient in many ways, but I find it damned near impossible to work with her. . . . No, don't bother finding me anyone else. I shan't be staying here much longer, and I'll see to it personally when I come down to Sydney. . . . No, I don't think Diane will be back, unfortunately. She's gone back to London. Her mother's in hospital, but apart from that, she wasn't happy away from Europe. The heat was giving her health problems. . . . Yes, I'll be lucky to find anyone to suit me so well. What I need is someone mature, who won't bug me with her private life and has plenty of interests apart from sex. . . . Sure, I'll let you know when I'm coming. It will be great to see you again. . . . Thanks for your concern, but I've changed my plans about staying here. How's Shay? . . . Oh, I won't hold it against her. . . . Yes, I'll be seeing you both shortly, Good-bye."

He hung up and Aidan stood staring into space. Her cheeks were burning and she was trembling slightly. So he found it "damned near" impossible to work with her. It was the first she'd heard of it, and she felt deeply hurt. She'd thought that at least her efficiency in dealing with his difficult manuscript had satisfied him. As for his insinuations that she bugged him and hadn't any interests apart from sex—what sort of impression must that have given Michael?

She discovered he was standing in the doorway, his

bare chest dark above a pair of white jeans, and she looked at him accusingly.

"I don't want lunch," he said, ignoring her expression. "If I do, I'll fix something myself." He sent her one long, intense look and then turned away. A moment later she heard the study door shut firmly.

I hate you, she thought passionately. But the tears that filled her eyes had nothing to do with hatred.

That afternoon she immersed herself in her work, and later, when she took a break, she went down to the beach and swam. Hoping, of course, that he'd come and join her. But he didn't. And over dinner, when at last he emerged from his seclusion and joined her, he had so little to say that she kept quiet too. If his work were troubling him, she didn't want to do or say anything that would upset him. And though she longed to ask him when he was planning to go to Sydney, she didn't dare.

Three days went by during which she saw him only at dinnertime. He left fresh work for her each morning in her office, and if he had any comments or requests, he wrote them and left them for her. She didn't go to the resort. She was restless and moody, and when she took a break it was to swim or to gather flowers and arrange them in bowls for the house—something he never commented on, so she doubted if he even noticed it. She was more and more aware that he had something on his mind. His work, she kept telling herself. It must be going badly.

But was it his work? Or was it something to do with her? And then she was back in a never-ending circle of speculation. Was he annoyed because their relationship had flowed over into a forbidden channel? Was that why he found her impossible to work with. Yet whose fault had it been? Hadn't *he* been the one to bring sex into it in the first place—even if she had then responded to him too emotionally for his liking?

The thought of returning to Sydney, of never seeing him again, spurred her on as nothing else could have to please him with her work. Which was laughable. He'd never in a million years employ her permanently as his secretary. In any case, she wasn't altogether sure she'd want him to.

Vanda arrived at the bungalow one afternoon, demanding to see Guy.

"I'm sorry, he's working," Aidan told her. She'd abandoned her own work half an hour ago and was in the garden with a book, pretending to read.

Vanda looked as if she'd like to shake her. "It's five o'clock; the day's over. No one can work all day. I have to see him."

"Why?" Aidan demanded implacably.

"That's none of your business. It's something between me and Guy. You had your little hour the other night when Guy had been drinking—but don't let it go to your head."

She made a sudden move toward the bungalow, and Aidan jumped to her feet and confronted her. For a few seconds the two girls stood staring at each other with hostility. Like animals about to have a fight, Aidan thought, feeling more than slightly sick. She told Vanda shakily, "Please Vanda—it's more than my job's worth to let you disturb Guy. You know he hates to be interrupted. You know he'll be angry. With you as well as with me."

"Leave me out of it," Vanda snapped back. "I'm not an employee. I have special privileges. Haven't you caught on to that yet?"

Aidan clenched her fists. "No, I'm afraid I haven't.

Guy's never instructed me that you were an exception in any way to the orders he's given me. I'm not going to let you disturb him."

Silence. In her heart, Aidan really believed that Vanda was going to attack her. Instead, the other girl stared at her, her brown eyes blazing.

"I told you once that if you tried to come between me and Guy, I'd make you sorry. You're not going to win, you know. Not any more than Diane did. Just you wait and see."

With one more vindictive look, she turned on her heel and walked away, and Aidan felt her body sag.

Chapter Seven

The following day seemed to Aidan to be unbearably hot and oppressive. There'd been a thunderstorm during the night, and it looked as if another one was blowing up that afternoon. She decided to knock off work for an hour or so and take a swim in the hope of cooling down. Still, perhaps her troubles were more psychological than anything else. She was far from happy working under the present conditions, scarcely seeing Guy, exchanging no more than a few words with him when they did meet. Anything would be better than that. She'd sooner he was complaining about her, reviling her—anything at all.

As she swam lazily in the water, she thought of him continually, wishing he'd come and join her. She longed just to hear his voice, to look into his eyes. It was madness, of course, and her reason told her it would be a good thing when he decided to leave the island and her time with him was ended. She'd thought sometimes of asking him exactly what Michael had said about her, but she'd had no business listening to that telephone conversation, since it was a private call. A good secretary simply didn't do that kind of thing. Or if she did, then she acted as if she'd heard nothing.

She came out of the water at last and began to walk toward the shade of the palms. Her tiny bikini was already beginning to dry in the heat of a sun that was growing hazy with heavy clouds, and as she shook back her wet hair and ran her fingers through it, she saw with a shock that Guy had come down from the bungalow and was only a few yards from her. Guilt flooded over her automatically at the darkly brooding look on his face, and she wondered if someone had come—and she hadn't been at her post to play dragon.

"I'm sorry . . . were you looking for me, Mr. Desailley?" she stammered, halting a few paces from him, acutely aware that he was watching her intently. It sounded absurd to call him Mr. Desailley, and yet her tongue refused to say his name—Guy. It was as if by saying it, she might give herself away somehow. But she couldn't stop her eyes from feasting on him—on his dark, curling hair, the sheen of his thick eyelashes, the mobile line where his lips met, on the muscular strength of his bare chest. She discovered suddenly that she was staring at him bemusedly and hadn't heard what he was saying to her.

"I'm sorry," she said again. "I . . . it was so hot, I thought I'd take a swim before it stormed. I'm nearly through the work you left me anyhow. Is everything all right?"

He didn't bother answering a question so obviously foolish, but told her, "I said Brian brought some mail over from the lodge."

"Oh! I suppose I should have been there," she

exclaimed, flushing. "I'm sorry you had to leave your work."

He gave a slightly twisted smile. "Such concern! Do you really care all that much?"

Her colour deepened still further. They'd begun walking toward the bungalow and she said a little heatedly, "What do you mean? I've been right there on the spot for the past several days, and nobody's come. Only the girl to do the cleaning. And Vanda. But perhaps you wanted to see her," she added challengingly.

"If I had, I'd have come outside. I'd have had to be deaf not to hear the two of you talking. And for heaven's sake, don't apologise for *that*," he said, as she turned toward him, her lips already parted to do just that. "Every second word you've uttered so far has been an apology. I'm beginning to wonder what's the matter with you."

"Maybe *I'm* beginning to be aware that I make a lot of mistakes. That I'm . . ." she paused, but she couldn't keep it in, and she finished vehemently, ". . . I'm impossible to work with."

"Is that rankling?" he said sardonically. "Well, listeners are supposed never to hear any good of themselves. . . . There's a letter for you at the house, by the way, though I'm afraid it's not from your fiancé. Not that I imagine you're all that eager to hear from him, judging by the way you've been putting in your spare time on the island. What's happened that you haven't been dashing off to meet your holiday lover lately, anyhow? I've been a little alarmed at how you've been sticking so discreetly to the bungalow. Ever since the night we took that swim together, in fact."

She bit her lip and looked at the ground, praying desperately that he wouldn't notice how her face was burning. But of course he *was* looking at her, and even though she was wearing her bikini, she felt somehow naked. She had a vision of herself walking up the beach towards him with not a stitch on. Out of pure self-defence she began to hurry ahead without making any answer to his remarks.

As she started up the verandah steps, he called after her, "Your mail's in your bedroom, Aidan."

Aidan. He seemed to say it so caressingly. But that was all in her imagination, she reminded herself bitterly.

In her room, she sank down on the bed, pushing her hair out of her eyes. It was heavy with salt, and she longed to get under the shower. Her letter, as she'd suspected, was from Shay, but as she ripped it open, her mind was only half on it. She was listening for Guy, and it was not until she heard the door of his study slam shut that she began to read what her cousin had written.

There were a few preliminaries, and then Shay apologised for having allowed Michael to telephone Guy.

"Aidan, I had no idea it was in his mind. He just said nothing when I told him you'd gone up north to work for Guy, and then without giving me a chance to explain that you really could do all the things he'd expect of a secretary, he went straight to the telephone. And there was just no *point*. A man like Guy doesn't need to be nursemaided. How *have* you been getting on with him, Aidan? All Michael will say is that you're too young. But so long as you're efficient, I can't see that age matters a row of beans, I really can't. And—isn't he a dish???!!!"

Aidan raised her eyes from the hastily scrawled page. Was Guy "a dish"? All she knew was that she'd been mad enough to fall in love with him—and that he didn't even believe in love. Yet he had only to touch her and she was set on fire. It shamed her.

With an effort, she returned to Shay's letter.

"Anyhow, I expect you'll want to hear about Sylvia's house. Michael's had a couple of offers for it that he wouldn't even consider. He said it wasn't worthwhile bothering you with them—you wouldn't want to let the property go for a song just to line the pocket of some speculator. Personally, I still think Aunt Sylvia should have left money to the kids, and the house to you. It was your home, and it's such a warm and lovely old house despite the crazy architecture. (Robert could have remedied that!) And the view is priceless.

"I gather Guy means to come to Sydney fairly soon— and that you'll be looking for work again. Well, just don't worry about a thing, Aidan. You're welcome to stay with us as long as you like. See you! Love, Shay."

Darling Shay! She was a real friend. Smiling, Aidan folded the letter, put it back in the envelope and went into the shower.

An hour and a half later she had Guy's dinner ready, but he didn't appear. The storm had arrived, rain thudded on the roof, and the bungalow grew hot and steamy.

She waited awhile. The last few nights, Guy had appeared at about seven o'clock, and they'd eaten together in the living room—mainly in silence. Tonight, she waited until seven thirty and then she dished up his meal, loaded it on a tray and carried it to his study. After all, he had to eat.

"Here's your dinner, Mr. Desailley."

She stood just inside the room, and he turned round from his desk and looked at her.

"Take it away, for goodness' sake. If I want a meal, I'll come out and sit down to it. Surely you know that by now. I'm not hungry."

He turned his back on her and fuming, she carried the tray out of the room, kicking the door shut after her and hearing it slam with a feeling of childish satisfaction.

She wasn't hungry either. The weather was enervating, and the storm seemed to have set her nerves on edge. She merely toyed with the steak she had cooked, and then made herself some coffee. She just didn't know why she imagined she was in love with a man like that, she reflected as she sat alone at the table. He was so temperamental, so unpredictable. She could tell herself a hundred times that writers were like that; that even Sylvia had been touchy when she was having problems with her work. But it didn't make her feel any happier.

Presently she went onto the verandah to sit and watch the silver rain falling in the dark garden and listen to the frogs croaking and the leaves of the palms rattling. And to wonder what it would be like to be married to Guy Desailley. He'd been married once. Shay had told her that, and she'd gathered he'd been shattered by his wife's death. Now, for some reason, he no longer believed in love. Yet Vanda Hardy seemed convinced he was going to marry her. Frankly, Aidan thought that would be a disaster. From what she'd seen, Vanda didn't have much understanding of the psychology of a writer, and though Aidan fancied that she herself had learned quite a bit during the years she'd lived with her aunt, she still couldn't pretend even she understood Guy.

Meanwhile, he professed himself proof against falling in love. So where did that leave either of them? She, in fact, had no more chance of marrying him than Vanda had. For all she knew, her chances were even less, and the best thing she could do was to forget him. If she could.

Determinedly, she went to her bedroom and fetched her writing pad. She'd answer Shay's letter. That would be better than moping over her impossible love for Guy. Of which she was going to say not one word to Shay. She was going to start pretending it didn't exist, because obviously there was no future in it. Guy had shown her very plainly that she meant nothing to him; yet to her despair, no matter how much she reasoned with herself, there was something in her that simply refused to accept the inevitable. She had only to think of the warmth and passion of his kisses, of a certain tenderness that seemed undeniable, and she was ready to be persuaded that if a man kissed you that way, then you must mean something to him.

And *she* must be the most naïve and gullible girl that had ever come into Guy Desailley's life, she reminded herself with sudden realism. She was doing exactly what he'd accused her of doing: romanticising. And she'd better keep in mind that love didn't exist for him. It did for her, though, she reflected bitterly, and from her brief knowledge of it, it must be the most agonising of all the so-called pleasurable emotions.

With an effort, she turned to her letter and sat, pen in hand, wondering what she'd tell Shay.

She soon discovered it was almost impossible to write to her cousin and to mention Guy only in an impersonal way, and she made several attempts before she was in any way satisfied. There was nothing to apologise about, she assured Shay, and she wouldn't be in the least sorry to hand over her job to someone else. "We just don't get on," she wrote—a meaningless phrase under the circumstances, and one that would probably disappoint her cousin, who thought Guy such a dish.

Somewhere along the line, it occurred to her that it was going to be very awkward indeed to move in with the Hamiltons again in Sydney knowing that Guy, as a close friend of Michael's, was likely to be invited to their home quite frequently. What hope would she have of forgetting him under those circumstances? she asked herself in dismay.

With sudden inspiration she wrote, "Thanks for your generous offer of a home, but I might stop off in Brisbane, since I'm up this way, and look for work there. I want to steer clear of Robert for a while longer—break the circuit—and if Michael wouldn't mind carrying the burden of disposing of the house, I'd be truly grateful."

She added a few general remarks about the beauty of the island and then scrawled her name and with a sigh of relief tucked the letter away in its envelope.

The storm was still rumbling outside, and there seemed nothing to do now except go to bed. A little reluctantly, she gathered up her writing materials and went inside to her room, noting with a slight pang that Guy was still shut away in his study. Why did he find her so impossible to work with, she wondered as she sank down on the side of her bed and stared into space. She really didn't think she was as bad as all that. She didn't find *him* impossible to work with, despite his unpredictability. What did disturb her—and her efficiency, if she didn't watch it—was her own emotional reaction to him. She didn't know whether Diane had had the same problem or not. According to Vanda, she might well have.

After a few minutes of giving in to her feelings of restlessness and frustration, she went into the living room and selected a book to read, more or less at random. A really old book, called *The Pelican Pool*. On the fly leaf was written 'Martha Desailley,' and it gave her a curious pleasure to think it had probably belonged to Guy's grandmother. The pages were spotted

126

with rust marks and the story was weirdly old-fashioned, as she discovered when she got into bed and began to read.

The book had fallen from her hands and she was just about asleep when someone knocked on the door and Guy's voice asked, "Are you awake, Aidan?"

She sat up abruptly, her heart thumping.

"Yes—what is it?" Still half asleep, she slid her feet to the floor and stumbled to the door. Guy stood there, his hands on his narrow hips, the gold chain gleaming against his bare chest. His dark glance went rapidly over her slim form, its outline clearly visible through the flimsy cotton of her nightdress. She wrapped her arms around herself hastily, and he smiled wryly, his eyes returning to her face.

"Come and fix me something to eat, Aidan," he said.

"What? Now?" She gaped at him foolishly, her grey eyes wide.

"Well, of course now. I'm hungry. I can't go to bed on an empty stomach, and I'm not going to swallow down a slice of bread and butter in a solitary state in the kitchen. I want you to get into some clothes and come out. Right?"

She nodded speechlessly, and he turned and strode away.

Once he'd gone, she scrambled quickly into jeans and a T-shirt, not bothering to put on a bra. She brushed her hair at the mirror and listened to the rain, seeming to hear another sound behind it—the throbbing of her own heart. Excitement had risen in her headily, and she refused to ask herself why.

When she went to the kitchen, barefoot, he was there leaning against the table, a can of beer in his hand.

"What would you like?" she asked, unnerved by the way he was looking at her.

His expression changed swiftly, and she knew he'd chosen to put a different interpretation on her question from the one she'd intended. She felt her body trembling, and she moistened her lips nervously, yet she couldn't look away from him.

"What would I like?" His brows rose quizzically, and his glance moved over her slowly, taking in the soft curve of her breast under the cotton shirt and finally coming to rest on her mouth.

He stopped there, and her mind flew into confusion. *Did* his words have a double meaning or was it all in her mind?

"There's some cold chicken," she said shakily, trying to ignore any possible innuendoes. "And I can make you a salad. Or would you like me to cook you a steak?"

"Cold chicken will suit me fine." His voice was ironic, and he took a long draught of beer. Aidan turned away and went to the fridge, and as she set the chicken and salad vegetables on the counter she asked, "I'll bring it into the living room when it's ready, shall I?"

"Do that," he agreed. "And you can come in and keep me company while I eat."

"Very well," she said coolly, though she felt far from cool.

He left her alone to fix his meal, and she went to some trouble to make an attractive salad, buttered some thin slices of bread, added pepper and salt and mayonnaise and another can of beer to the tray she was loading up; then she carried the lot inside. She knew it was absurd of her to feel so excited, so stimulated, as she deposited the tray on a table near the chair he'd chosen.

"You've made a positive work of art of that salad,"

he remarked, raising his eyebrows in surprise as he helped himself to it. "It's more than I deserve after hauling you out of bed at this hour."

"I don't really mind," she said, sitting down and looking at him through her lashes. "After all, you did tell me when I first came that I could expect to be called on to do anything and everything at any hour of the day or night. And so far, I can't honestly say you've made any demands on me that . . . that I haven't expected."

"I haven't? You really feel that? Well, you're taking a very lenient view of my . . . misdemeanours tonight. It's a pleasant change."

She flushed slightly and leaned back in her chair so her face was no longer in the light of the lamp. She found his scrutiny of her disconcerting, to say the least, and his unreadable inky-blue eyes had scarcely left her alone since she'd come into the room.

"You've been having problems the last few days, haven't you, Mr. Desailley?" she suggested.

He frowned. "Call me Guy, for goodness sake. . . . What problems do you think I've been having, Aidan?"

"To do with your work," she said promptly. "I know, because my aunt used to strike rough patches now and again. I could usually tell when it was happening, and I'd try any way I could to make things easier for her. Oh, I know I can't do much to help *you*," she babbled on. "What you really need is a wife—someone who'll be there to listen to you whenever you want to talk, to . . ." She broke off abruptly, flinching at the sudden hardness of his expression.

"You don't know the first thing about my needs, Miss Elliot," he said coldly. "I've been getting by without a wife for some time now, so don't try to make plans for me."

"I wasn't making plans for you," she protested. "I

129

only said you need a wife. Then you wouldn't have to get your secretary out of bed at eleven o'clock at night to talk to you—to make you a meal."

He put his plate, his meal only partly eaten, onto the tray and looked at her through narrowed eyes.

"You have marriage on the brain, Aidan. I knew it the first time we met. You're not by any chance suggesting you'd make me a suitable wife, are you?"

"Of course I'm not!" she exclaimed, blushing crimson. "I . . ."

"Merely because I happen to have made a couple of harmless passes at you?" he pursued relentlessly, breaking in on her embarrassed protest.

Harmless passes! Was that how he saw his lovemaking? Aidan couldn't believe it.

"You seem to have forgotten I'm already engaged," she flared.

"No, I haven't forgotten," he said laconically, and reached for the can of beer she'd brought in. "But it seems to have slipped *your* mind once or twice since you've been here. I'm surprised your fiancé hasn't written to you. Have you had a quarrel, by any chance? Or do you believe in allowing each other the right to lead separate personal lives?"

"Robert's working on a rather big project at the moment, as it happens," she retorted, a little shocked at her own glibness. "He just doesn't have time to write unnecessary letters."

"Unnecessary? To the woman he loves?" His mouth twisted wryly. "I don't think even I should be all that sanguine if I were the man in the case and you the girl. I'm surprised to find you so matter-of-fact when it comes to affairs of the heart. I wouldn't have expected it of you, Aidan. I only hope Robert's as tolerant of you. Though I suppose he hasn't an inkling of what you've been up to on this island." Aidan bit her lip and said nothing, and he concluded irritatingly, "All the same, if I were you, I'd take care not to go too far."

That was funny coming from him, she reflected, as she told him calmly, "I'm not likely to do that. Anyhow you're planning to leave here soon, aren't you?"

"Am I?" His brows lifted. "I don't recall discussing my plans with you."

"No, you didn't," she agreed, smarting. "You prefer to leave me in the dark. Do you think that's fair? I know I'm only your secretary, but I happen to be a human being as well."

"Oh, I know that, Aidan," he said sardonically. "In fact, it's becoming only too obvious that you and I are very well aware of each other as human beings. Of the opposite sex," he added. "Hence, your little talk of my needing a wife."

She bit her lip and said the first thing that came into her head. "I was thinking of Vanda, not myself."

"*Vanda?*" He set the beer can down and stared at her in amazement. "When did I ever suggest I'd even consider marrying Vanda? Didn't I hear you telling her only the other day that she wasn't an exception to my orders not to let anyone interrupt me?"

"I said that to stop her from bursting in on you," Aidan said. She was beginning to feel exhausted by this verbal sparring. "I . . . I have no idea how you feel about her. But . . . well, you own this island and her parents run the resort, and you have known Vanda for a long time, haven't you? So you see . . ."

"I don't see a thing," he said dryly. "You're talking a lot of rubbish."

"But I'm not! I know that a writer's life is lonely. You must need someone to . . ."

"Oh, for God's sake, I've heard enough of your drivel, Aidan," he interrupted. "You don't know what you're talking about. Loneliness is something one learns to live with, and I have no intention of rushing into marriage with anyone. I know damned well a woman can be more hindrance than help, with her constant and insatiable demands. All I need is a good, sensible secretary. The kind of relationship I had with Diane suited me perfectly. We worked together very amicably without the complications of sex."

Aidan listened skeptically. Vanda had told her something very different about Diane, and she asked flatly, "Why don't you try to get her to come back, then?"

He shrugged his broad shoulders. "She has her own life to live. I had a letter from her today, as a matter of fact. Her mother's recovering, and she's found herself another job in London, so that's that. I daresay I'll find someone who'll suit me just as well if I take my time over it."

"I'm not in the running, of course," Aidan remarked without really meaning to.

"Definitely not." His eyes flicked over her slim figure as she leaned back in the armchair, and she could feel the rise and fall of her breasts as his glance lingered on them. She wished futilely that she'd taken the time to put on a bra, instead of being in such a hurry to dress and rush out to him.

Suddenly he got up from his chair, slammed the beer can down on the tray and paced the length of the room and back, then stood staring down at her narrowly.

"Do you look at every man you meet like that, Aidan? Those damned come-to-bed eyes of yours distract me every time I encounter them. And that, if you want to know, is why I find you so impossible to work with."

Aidan's eyes widened with shock. Did she look at him the way he said? She felt the colour rush to her face and then subside, leaving her pale.

He continued to stare at her broodingly. "I don't

know how much Shay told you about my marriage, Aidan—or even how much she knows. But it was an experience I don't intend to repeat. I married young, and I married for love, and it was hell. I was trying to find my feet as a writer, and Lenore couldn't come to terms with the life I had to lead. She wanted everything at once—right away. Anything I did that didn't put her in a starring role in my life, she was jealous of. Our marriage was on the rocks in no time—while I worked, she went out with other men. She had no trouble finding herself admiring escorts who'd give her the good time she wanted. She was a very beautiful girl." He stopped, a bitter smile twisting his mouth, and then added unexpectedly, "But not as beautiful as you are, Aidan."

Unexpectedly, he crouched down in front of her, reaching out to grip her hands in his. Aidan's heart seemed to leap into her throat, and her hands trembled under the pressure of his. She realised with some part of her mind that the storm was over, yet inside the air seemed laden with electricity. She looked into Guy's face, trying to take in what he'd said, trying to decide what it meant—if anything. She knew she was no match for this man, who was more practised in the art of seduction than any other man she'd ever encountered.

When he straightened up and pulled her to her feet, she didn't resist. He held her a little away from him, his eyes searching hers disconcertingly.

"You're planning to marry soon, are you?"

"I . . . I don't know," she stammered, not knowing what to say. She gasped as he drew her fiercely against him, crushing her body to his.

"I should never have let you stay here," he muttered against her hair. "You've ruined my peace of mind—my habits of work."

"But why?" she whispered, aware of her wildly

beating heart. "I've tried to help . . . to understand . . . to . . . to leave you alone. I haven't in-
truded . . ."

He laughed—a brief, bitter sound. "Haven't you?
I've done nothing for a week. Nothing but sit at my
desk and think of you."

The words were half smothered as his lips brushed
her brow, and she wondered afterward if she'd imagined them. Before she was aware of what was happening, his mouth had descended on hers and he was
kissing her with a kind of fierce yet gentle desperation,
his lips caressing, his hands moving urgently from her
arms to find the swell of her soft breast.

"Why do you let me do this?" he muttered against
the corner of her mouth. One hand had pushed her
shirt aside and she felt his fingers warm and seeking
against her flesh, as her body relaxed limp and helpless
against his male hardness. He pulled her down on the
sofa, and she went with him as if her body were welded
to his, to lie trembling as his bulk covered her, and his
kisses grew more and more passionate, more irresistible.

She no longer seemed to have a separate will of her
own, her mind had gone curiously, blissfully blank. All
she wanted was that he should go on kissing her. She
didn't care why he was doing it; it was enough that he
wanted to make love to her and that she wanted it to
happen. Her blood ran fast, she could feel it racing
through her veins, and she laid her cheek against the
hardness of his bare chest, feeling the roughness of hair
against her smooth skin, her legs twining themselves
with his. He kissed her mouth, her eyelids, and then
returned to her lower lip, soft and warm to his tongue,
and she heard him breathe her name. "Aidan."

"Guy," she whispered back. And then, as she'd
begged once before, "Kiss me—kiss me—"

He kissed her once more, briefly and searingly, and then he drew away from her. She seized his arm and tried to pull him back to her, while a voice that she realised dimly was her own implored him huskily, "Don't stop—don't go away—"

He didn't answer. He'd got to his feet and stood with his back to her and she could hear his deep, slow breathing before he told her thickly, "I'm not coming back, Aidan. I've had enough. I'm going out."

She sat up, pushing back her tumbled hair and feeling confused and disoriented, not knowing what this was all about, not understanding him, knowing only that she loved him and wanted to tell him so.

"Guy," she said painfully. "About Robert . . . I . . ."

He turned round swiftly, his face contorted with some emotion that she couldn't understand. "I don't want to hear about Robert. I don't want to hear your excuses. I don't damned well want to get involved with you. Do you understand?"

They stared at each other for a long moment and in the darkness of his eyes she could read nothing. It was as though he didn't even see her. Then, as she stumbled to her feet and put a hand to her burning lips, he turned away from her and left the room.

She heard the screen door slam as he went through to the verandah, and then the house was empty. For a moment she stood staring at the door. Her first instinct was to follow him, to force him to listen to her, to tell him that she wasn't going to marry Robert, that *he* was the one she loved.

Instead she forced herself to stay where she was. She'd run after him the night they went into the sea, and that had obviously been a mistake. It might amuse him—God knows why—to stir her up, but as he'd just told her so forcibly, he didn't want to get involved with her. He'd probably go berserk if she told him she loved him. It was the last thing he wanted.

She was beginning to understand vaguely why that was, since he'd talked about his marriage. Yet surely it was wrong to judge all women by one. If she were married to him, she'd be content to take second place to his work. Just so long as she knew he loved her, just so long as she could sleep in his arms at night, bear his children—if he wanted children . . .

But she was crazy.

She pulled herself together, gathered up the dishes and carried them out to the kitchen. She might as well face up to the fact that she was in a hopeless situation. She could tell herself a thousand times that *she'd* understand Guy and his needs, that she wouldn't try to compete with his work, but he'd made up his mind to take no more chances, and he wasn't going to marry again. Women—apart from an efficient and preferably sexless secretary—had only one place in his life, and that was to satisfy his sexual needs. Aidan knew very well he had far too passionate a nature to live like a monk, and that he also had enormous self-control. Possibly he exercised it out of consideration for her, but it was driving her mad.

She left the dishes in the sink and went back to her bed, to lie there exhausted and wakeful. She was disturbingly aware of the fact that for the first time in her life, she wanted a man to make love to her. She wanted it badly. So why did he always break off, leave her, control himself? *Was* it out of consideration for her? Or was it because he didn't want to be so closely involved with a woman who was sharing the bungalow with him? Or was it because he believed she was engaged to another man? Perhaps if she told him the truth about Robert . . .

Lying on her side, staring unseeingly at the dim

shape of the windows, she thought of those words he'd murmured as his lips caressed her skin: "I've done nothing for a week but sit at my desk and think of you." Exactly what did that mean? She wished she knew. Yet even if she told him about Robert, that wasn't going to make him fall in love with her, want her to marry him.

More confused than ever, she fell asleep at last.

Chapter Eight

Guy was nowhere around the next morning when she got up.

It was late, and she thought perhaps he'd gone out fishing, until the girl who came to do the cleaning asked cheerfully, "Has Mr. Desailley gone on one of his walkabouts?"

Aidan's spirits sank like lead. Had he done that—after last night and its frustrations?

Her cheeks reddening at the direction her thoughts were taking, she went back to her typewriter and tried to get on with the work he'd left for her the day before and that she hadn't finished yet.

Once the cleaning girl had gone, the silence and emptiness of the bungalow became oppressive. Aidan couldn't keep her mind off Guy. Where had he gone? And why hadn't he told her, or at least left a written message for her, saying he'd be out for the day? Or for two days—any kind of message at all.

Maybe he was making arrangements to leave the island and go back to Sydney. He'd said he couldn't work with her around. If he turned up this evening, it could be with tickets in his pocket and instructions for her to pack her things.

She couldn't work for thinking of him. By afternoon, the waste basket was filled with pages she'd spoiled and had to discard, and her thoughts simply refused to stay on what she was doing. She remembered Louise Hardy's warning that she was storing up trouble for herself, and she hated to have to admit that the woman had been right. She should never have come here. That way she'd never have met him. But since she had come—well, how do you stop yourself from falling in love, anyhow? It seemed to Aidan that it was like falling off a cliff. Once it had happened, there was nothing you could do about it.

Unless you were Guy Desailley, of course. He simply chose not to fall in love with anyone, and so it didn't happen. Certainly not with Aidan Elliot.

The day went by with unbelievable slowness. Somehow, she knew he wouldn't be back, yet just the same, she waited and waited for him, and even after she went to bed, she lay wakeful, listening. If he had come, no matter how quietly, she'd have heard him.

But he didn't come, and eventually she slept.

Predictably, Vanda turned up at the door the next afternoon, ready to push her way into Guy's study.

"He's not there," Aidan said, and Vanda tossed back her blond hair and looked at her unbelievingly. "He's been away since yesterday. Didn't you notice the boats are missing?"

Vanda stared and began to smile. "I do believe you're put out!" she exclaimed. "Though if you understood the least little thing about Guy, you wouldn't be surprised. He's always unpredictable when he's working. He gets moody, he needs to be alone, and he goes to walkabout. Did you think with you around he'd stay put? Or are you looking so disagreeable because he didn't tell you where he was going or how long he'd be away?"

Aidan raised her eyebrows and tried to look unconcerned. "Am I looking disagreeable? Maybe that's just because I never seem to enjoy your company much, Vanda."

Vanda blinked, then recovered quickly. "Diane didn't enjoy my company either. Well, since you feel that way about me, I'll leave you to wallow in your gloom. It's a pity you're so determined to make a fool of yourself over Guy. If you had any sense, you'd come over to the resort and enjoy yourself."

"Thank you for the suggestion, but I'm not making a fool of myself. It just happens I have a lot of work to do here," Aidan said stiffly.

"Oh, dear, aren't you virtuous?" The other girl sneered. "Guy must be so impressed by your conscientiousness." She had perched herself on the verandah rail, and she swung one long, slim brown leg. "But don't you think it just might be your . . . unremitting devotion to duty that's driven him away?"

Aidan clenched her fists. "I'll leave all the speculating to you, Vanda. I'm going back to my work. Is there some book you want to borrow before you leave?"

"No, thanks." Vanda refused to rise to the gibe. "I just wandered over to say hello and see what was happening in this neck of the woods."

"Then I hope you're satisfied with what you've found out."

"Oh yes, I'm quite satisfied." With a smug smile, Vanda slipped down from the rail and went down the steps.

Aidan watched her saunter off but she didn't go back to her typewriter. Instead, she changed into her bikini and spent the rest of the afternoon on the beach. Thinking of Guy. Thinking of what Vanda had said, knowing that it wasn't her "unremitting devotion to duty" that was responsible for Guy's disappearance, and that Vanda had meant a very different kind of devotion. Perhaps she'd even hit the nail on the head.

Sitting hunched up on the sand, her face in her hands, she let out a shuddering breath. It was plain crazy to be in love with him. It would be better to hate him—to hate him for stirring her up so callously and so casually, and then dropping her as if she were of no importance.

So she'd try to hate him. And when he came back, he'd find her very different. She'd never lose control of herself again. It didn't pay. If any vanishing was to be done, then she'd be the one to do it. And that would be if he tried to touch her again. She'd pack her bags. She'd leave.

And she didn't believe one word of what she was telling herself.

Three more long days dragged by. Somehow she blundered her way through the work Guy had left for her, though she was a mass of nerves. With nothing left to do, she wandered through the empty bungalow moodily. Why didn't she use her head and forget Guy? Vanda, though she hated to admit it, had been right. She should walk over to the resort and enjoy herself. Look up Steve. His holiday must be just about over by now, and she really owed him an apology for not turning up on the beach as she'd promised that night when Guy had carried her off so high-handedly. Goodness knows what sort of opinion he must have of her now. As Louise Hardy had said, "What do you suppose people will think when they know you're living alone at the bungalow with a man?"

Though Steve, she persuaded herself, wouldn't think things. He was too nice a person.

All the same, she didn't go over to the resort. Instead, she went down to the beach to swim.

As she came back to the bungalow, she heard the telephone ringing. She ran to answer it, sure that it must be Guy, but the ringing had stopped by the time she reached the door.

"Damn," she exclaimed aloud, tears of frustration in her eyes. She didn't dare go to the shower in case the phone rang again. It wasn't until six o'clock, when she knew no more outside calls would be coming to the island, that she gave up. Why would he telephone her, anyhow? She probably wasn't even in his mind.

Next morning she really took herself in hand. Over a meager breakfast, she made up her mind to walk round to the resort to see Steve. To straighten things out, to apologise, to say good-bye. She wouldn't hurry back. If Steve asked her to stay for a swim, to have a game of tennis—anything at all—then she'd do that. She'd spend the whole day at the resort. And she hoped rather childishly that Guy would come back and find her gone.

She changed into her green bikini, stepped into white shorts and pulled a sun top over her head. Then she stowed underthings and her tan crinkle-cotton dress in a beach bag and set off for the resort.

By a stroke of good luck, she caught sight of Steve ahead of her as she wandered in the direction of the pool. Quickening her step, she caught up with him and touched his arm.

"Hello, Steve. Remember me?"

He turned toward her with obvious embarrassment. "Hello, Aidan. What are you doing here? I thought you were much too occupied to bother with me these days."

She writhed inwardly at his skeptical tone. "I have been busy," she said awkwardly. "I . . . it hasn't been easy to get away. I'm really sorry about that morning I was supposed to meet you. I thought you might have come over to the bungalow sometime," she improvised as he said nothing. He'd begun to walk on and she walked with him, and now he looked at her with a cynical smile.

"Did you? Well, I had the distinct idea that I wouldn't be welcome." He paused then added bluntly, "It seems a pretty funny sort of setup to me. From the few things you'd said about what you were doing I had the idea your boss was quite different. He's not exactly an old eccentric, is he. But that's none of my business, I suppose." They'd almost reached the pool now and he told her, "I'll have to leave you now. I'm meeting someone for a swim."

"That's okay," she said, flushing. "I came only to say good-bye and to apologise. You'll be leaving here soon, won't you?"

"Tomorrow, to be exact," he agreed.

"Well, good-bye, Steve," Aidan said. "It was nice meeting you." She smiled but he didn't reciprocate and with an almost offhanded "Good-bye," he strode on, leaving her alone.

She felt hurt, and even a little angry. She wanted to run after him and demand to know why he was so cool, what he thought of her. To protest her innocence.

She didn't, of course. With a sigh of exasperation she turned and walked swiftly away from the pool and the sight of the pretty girl obviously waiting for Steve. What was the use of protesting her innocence? Was she trying to clear her own conscience or something? She knew well enough that her relationship with Guy wouldn't have been innocent at all lately as if it had been left to her to make the choice. So maybe whatever Steve was thinking of her was right and she deserved it.

In a minute or so she discovered she'd nearly reached Reception and she slowed down. She had no desire at all to see Vanda or Louise Hardy. In fact, she was beginning to wonder why she'd come to the resort. To find Steve, she admitted, disillusioned with herself. To use him, to lean on him. To have him forgive her and ask her to spend the day with him. But he'd finished with her, and that was hardly surprising under the circumstances. So Aidan Elliot was on her own.

She was turning away when a poster caught her eye. It announced a day trip to the outer reef, departing at ten o'clock, tickets obtainable at the jetty. She glanced at her watch. Nine forty-five. Well, she might as well go. It would be a lot better than spending the day alone. And after all, it was madness to come all the way to North Queensland and not see the outer reef. And if Guy came back to the bungalow and wanted her, it would be just too bad for him.

She had her trip to the reef, and she actually managed to enjoy herself. She soon found herself teaming up with a young man called Neil, who had reddish hair, smudgy freckles and bright-blue eyes. She walked about on the reef with him, wearing sandshoes she'd rented on the launch. She snorkelled with him, and together they marvelled at the incredibly brilliant colouring of fish and corals seen close up. As they went back across the reef to the waiting launch for a late picnic lunch—late because the tide was all-important on a trip like this—she nearly slipped and Neil grabbed her and hugged her lightly. At that point, the thought of Guy began to bother her again.

On the homeward trip, Neil asked her if she had any

plans for the evening, and she mumbled vaguely that she didn't know.

"Hey, you're falling asleep!" he exclaimed. "Lean on my shoulder." He put his arm around her and pulled her against him. If his chest had been bare, she'd probably have struggled away from him, but he was respectably clad in a T-shirt so why not? She leaned her head on his shoulder, closed her eyes and pretended to go to sleep. Instead, she thought of Guy, and prayed hard that he'd come back today. She'd had enough of waiting. If he didn't come back, she was going to disappear. Somewhere along the line she'd reached that decision. She'd fly down to Brisbane and look for work. And she wouldn't even leave him a message. He'd have to guess where she'd gone. Though it mightn't even occur to him to wonder, for all she knew.

When the launch reached the jetty, she opened her eyes and yawned and managed to smile at the undemanding young man who'd given her such a quiet passage home.

"You look better," he said approvingly. "You needed that little nap. Now—how about dinner and dancing tonight?"

"I'd like that," she agreed at once.

"I'll see you in the bar, then. Half past seven?" he suggested jubilantly, and she nodded.

She parted from him with a wave of her hand on the jetty and began to hurry toward the white gate. Her heart was beating fast, and she wondered what she'd do if Guy were at the bungalow. Tell him she was leaving? She should, of course. But she didn't trust herself. She'd probably go weak at the knees and make a fool of herself.

He wasn't there. The bungalow was as deserted as it had been for the last few days and Aidan could have

wept with frustration. This thing had to be resolved.
Yet it was a thing that existed only in her own mind, she
told herself, trying to be sane, to be reasonable as, in
her bedroom, she stripped off her shirt and shorts, then
her bikini, and went into the bathroom to shower. Her
tears mingled with the lukewarm water as she soaped
herself and shampooed her hair, and she despised
herself utterly.

Why on earth had she told Neil that she'd come back
and have dinner with him? All she wanted, once she
stepped out from under the shower, was to get into
something comfortable, crawl into her bed and cry her
eyes out.

How could he do this to her? How *could* he? she
thought when, having towelled herself dry, she went
into her room and sat hunched in a chair, absentmindedly rubbing her wet hair with a towel and trying to
control the trembling of her mouth. Walking out on
her, leaving her, telling her absolutely nothing. And it
was no use at all reminding herself that she was nothing
more than an employee and that he didn't have to tell
her a thing. Wherever he was, whatever he was doing,
she was probably the last thing on his mind, and that
was what made it even more infuriating that she should
be here in his bungalow eating her heart out over him.

When her hair was dry, she dressed, choosing a
lipstick-red dress that she'd had for quite some time
and that had always been a favourite. It was very
simple, and with it she wore her wide, soft, gold belt
and gold sandals, and she clipped the flat gold rosette in
her hair. All the time she thought of Guy, trying to see
herself with his eyes as she looked in the big, heart-
shaped mirror. She took care with her makeup, using
soft grey-green eyeshadow to bring out the green in her
eyes and a brilliant lipstick that matched her dress.

She was going to be late, but she didn't hurry. All the

time she was listening, without being really conscious of it. Because he might come back.

Finally she could delay no longer. She found a flashlight and set off along the path through the ruined garden his parents had made long ago, walking slowly —just in case he should catch up to her and—oh, God, and take her in his arms and kiss her. *"Please, Guy,"* she heard herself say aloud, and tears rushed to her eyes.

She saw the resort lights ahead and pulled herself together. She really was becoming something of a nervous wreck, and that wasn't like her. She was usually so sane and sensible—or had been before she came to this island and met Guy. And fell in love. Who'd ever have thought love could make such a mess of anyone so quickly? It was really demoralising, and she was going to do something about it.

By the time she reached the bar, she was feeling better. Neil was waiting for her and looking rather anxious because she was so late. He smiled with relief when she arrived and she smiled back at him.

"Sorry I'm late. I had to wash my hair. It was just full of salt. I hope you haven't been waiting too long."

"That's okay. What would you like to drink?"

"Something exciting," she said. "You choose it for me."

It was exciting—and potent. By the time she'd had two drinks, she was feeling a lot more devil-may-care. She saw Steve across the room and waved to him gaily and then wanted to laugh at the look of surprise on his face when he saw Neil. Dinner was a tropical smorgasbord served in a big restaurant with its long unshuttered walls opening onto the night. There were strings of coloured lights through the garden, and beyond the palms the sea sparkled, the whole romantic effect heightened by soft music.

147

Neil ordered wine, and Aidan drank it recklessly, determined to keep her spirits high and her thoughts off Guy. By the time they'd finished eating and had drifted off to the dance floor, she didn't care much about anything.

Or so she told herself as she floated slowly about, Neil's arms supporting her, her cheek against his shoulder, her eyes closed. Trying hard not to pretend he was Guy.

They danced several times. Vanda came to the microphone to sing a couple of numbers and then disappeared. She'd seen Aidan, but after one sharp glance at Aidan's partner she'd turned away and not even acknowledged her. Aidan began to feel tired. She'd have told Neil she wanted to leave, except for the thought of the empty bungalow. Reluctantly, she agreed to dance again and drifted dizzily, her eyes closed, until something—she had no idea what—made her open them.

She found herself looking straight at Guy Desailley.

He was leaning against the doorframe halfway down the room. He wore close-fitting black pants, and his black shirt, open almost to the waist, revealed the glitter of his gold chain against the dark hairs on his chest. Aidan felt quite faint, but her eyes were wide open now and she couldn't take them off him. His jaw was dark, as if he badly needed a shave, and he stared back at her so intently, so compellingly, that she could feel her knees buckling, and she truly thought she was about to collapse.

Neil's arm tightened about her and he murmured something, but she had no idea what it was. As they danced they came closer and closer to where Guy stood watching. To Aidan it was unreal, as though she were taking part in some fantastic dream. Something was going to happen. She knew it because of the way Guy was looking at her.

Why was he looking at her like that? So—so hungrily, and as if he were angry too. Or was she imagining things? Was it some kind of wishful thinking—after all that alcohol she'd drunk?

Quite suddenly, Guy moved and his hand was on her bare shoulder, warm and hard, and then he pulled her roughly into his arms. He'd said something to Neil, but again she didn't seem capable of concentrating her attention on anything as demanding as words. She was quite sure that Guy had said nothing to her, hadn't even spoken her name, and now he was crushing her body to his in a way that didn't pretend to be anything but sexual. She knew, in fact, exactly how he was feeling, and her own desires rose in her like a flood so that she clung to him, her heart beating fast. She could feel his hand low on her back, pressing her against him, and he'd bent his head so he could look into her eyes.

She raised her face—the flower turning toward the sun—and looked back at him. Her bones seemed to melt; she felt the blood run hotly through her veins. Her lips parted softly and then he was kissing her—a long, long kiss, their lips clinging as they stood rocking together, scarcely moving. The lights had been lowered some time ago, and she had the feeling they were totally alone in an amber-coloured mist. She completely forgot about Neil and everyone else. Because Guy was here, and she was in his arms—the place where she most wanted to be in the whole world. When he took his mouth from hers, their eyes locked again and she could see the desire in his, and knew there was an unmistakable answer in her own.

For an eternity, they continued to stare at each other, their bodies moving rhythmically with the music, their eyes searching, asking, giving, in a way that seemed impossibly intimate and close. Aidan wanted to say "I love you," but the words remained in her heart.

Then something changed, his hand on her back relaxed, he glanced away from her, and she suddenly became conscious that they shouldn't be doing what they had been doing in public. Shouldn't have looked at each other the way they had, shouldn't have kissed, shouldn't have allowed their bodily contact to be so obviously—so blatantly—sexual.

She lowered her head. She wanted to ask him to take her away from here back to the bungalow where they could be alone.

Before she could bring herself to make the physical effort of speaking, the music had ended; his arm dropped from her and he walked away. Without a word. Aidan was staggered. She stared after him vacantly, and then it was as if she were waking out of a dream, discovering it had been just that, yet unable to adjust to reality. She was still following Guy with her eyes when she saw Vanda come toward him smiling, put her hand on his arm, and swing her blond hair back over her shoulder. They stood talking, and then began to dance as the music played again. Aidan felt a sickening spasm of jealousy shoot through her before someone touched her arm and she looked up, her eyes dark and dazed.

It was Neil. For a moment she couldn't even remember his name, and simply stared at him blankly.

"Going to dance with me again?" His glance was veiled, suspicious, but she nodded and let him swing her into his arms. He held her well away from him and asked her curiously, "Should I have let that guy dance with you? Do you know him?"

"Know him?" she repeated, feeling more than a little hysterical. "Yes, of course I know him. It didn't matter.

He was just . . ." Her voice trailed off and she discovered suddenly that she couldn't keep dancing. Her legs were trembling too much. She stood stock still. "I don't want to dance anymore, Neil. I'm tired. Do you mind if I go now?"

"It's up to you. Shall I walk you home?"

"No, don't bother," she said quickly. "I'll be all right. I don't want to spoil your evening." As she spoke she was searching for Guy and Vanda and not finding them. Instead, she caught Steve Guerney's eye. He looked speculative and not in the least friendly. She looked away quickly and with Neil escorting her, made her way among the dancing couples to the door.

"You're not feeling sick, or something, are you?" he asked, looking down at her pale face, and she shrugged and smiled faintly. "Too much sun, that's all. Thanks for a lovely evening, anyhow, Neil."

Outside, he let her go without suggesting they should meet again. And at that she couldn't be surprised—after the exhibition she and Guy had put on.

In the garden among the coloured lights she didn't hurry. She was still searching for Guy and Vanda, but they were nowhere to be seen, and again jealousy rose in her bitterly. Trembling, she began to run as if she had to escape from something.

When she reached the white gate she went through, but after taking only a few more steps, she collapsed against the trunk of a tree. She could hear the heavy painful beating of her heart and she had the feeling she was in a dark maze from which there was no way out. Why had he acted that way? Why had he—practically made love to her publicly and then simply walked away? Didn't he think she had any feelings? How could he treat her like that? The tears had begun streaming down her cheeks and she heard herself sob aloud. She hated him—hated him! She wished she'd never come

151

here, never met him. She'd been a fool to stay on these last few days. If she'd gone earlier, she'd be in the clear now—getting over him. Maybe away from this isolated island and its dreamlike beauty, its drugging heat, she'd have realised it was all no more than infatuation.

In the morning, she'd tell him she was leaving. And meanwhile, she'd better start moving. She didn't want him to catch her standing here weeping on his way back to the bungalow.

The path was dark and somewhere along the line she'd lost her flashlight. Inevitably, as she moved cautiously along, she remembered that other time when they'd walked along this path together and she'd ended up in his arms. She really had been all sorts of an idiot to let him get under her skin. But what kind of a man was he, for goodness' sake, to act the way he did? He didn't believe in love, he didn't want a personal relationship with his secretary, he even believed she was engaged to someone else. In fact, he didn't have to make love to her in any of the varied ways he'd chosen. If he wanted, he could just leave her alone. Tripping and stumbling and groping her way, her nostrils filled with the scent of frangipani flowers, she gradually made her way along the path.

She came through the last of the tall trees and saw lights ahead and blinked. Had she left the lights burning when she'd come out earlier? She was sure she hadn't. So he must be there—with Vanda. She shrank inwardly at the thought. What were they doing? Talking or . . . whatever. She finished the thought with a laugh that actually hurt.

Before she reached the door onto the back verandah she paused and slipped off her sandals; then, barefoot, she went quietly inside. She couldn't hear voices, and going through the breakfast annex, she reached the passage outside her bedroom. Thank goodness she didn't have to pass his room or the sitting room and that she had her own bathroom. She knew what she was going to do, and that was to start packing. Right away, so that tomorrow she'd be all ready to leave.

Still in her bright lipstick-red dress, and not daring to glance at her reflection, she began hauling her clothes from cupboards and drawers and packing them into her suitcase. She moved quietly, and though she couldn't hear any other sound in the house, she was still tensely conscious of the fact that he was there. Yet why were they so quiet? Was he there with Vanda? The suspense of not knowing was killing her, but nothing on earth would have persuaded her to go through the house and find out. It wouldn't be tactful, anyhow, she told herself bitterly. Besides, she had a strong feeling that after seeing her and Guy on the dance floor tonight, Vanda would feel like tearing her to shreds.

Footsteps. Her heart began to beat so hard, she thought it would burst. She knew it was Guy. She discovered she actually recognised the sound of his tread. She thrust down the lid of her suitcase and, leaving it on the bench, crossed to the door, reaching it at the same time as he did.

They looked at each other in silence. He still hadn't shaved and his eyes looked dark and mysterious; and she could see the heavy shadows under them. All her instincts urged her to reach out to him, to embrace him, to rest her head on his chest, to put her arms around him.

Instead, she asked him with an iciness that was frightening, "What do you want? Some coffee? Some supper?"

Chapter Nine

"No." His eyes searched hers darkly. "I thought I heard you, that's all."

She swallowed. "Well, now you know I'm here." She turned her back on him and began to walk into the room, but his hand shot out and he pulled her back.

"I want to talk to you, Aidan. You can come into the sitting room."

"But—isn't Vanda there?" she choked out, and his dark eyebrows arched.

"Why the hell would Vanda be there? Do you think she's my mistress?"

Aidan shook her head confusedly. "I . . . I thought you left with her after you'd been dancing."

"Then you thought wrong. I came back on my own. I've been waiting for you, in fact."

She twisted out of his grasp, and though she told herself she was not going into the sitting room to talk to him, that it was too risky, she went all the same. After all, she had things to tell him—such as that she'd packed her bag and was leaving tomorrow. And that she never wanted to see him again. A lie, of course, she reflected hopelessly.

One lamp glowed in the sitting room and the ceiling fan purred softly; otherwise it was unnervingly quiet.

"Sit down." He stood in the middle of the room, dark and handsome in his black pants and shirt. For once he wasn't bare-chested, and she felt an odd little relief at that. Somehow, he didn't seem so dangerous while he was fully clothed. Still, in her heart she knew he was every bit as dangerous, and in fact she'd had it proved to her tonight when they danced together. She sank down in a chair and leaned back, determined to relax, to stay in control of herself. But while he stood there looking at her the way he was doing she hadn't a hope of being in control of even one little finger. Even now her hands were twisting together, and she was staring back at him in exactly the way she didn't want to, though something he'd said to her before had come disconcertingly into her mind. "Those come-to-bed eyes of yours distract me every time I meet them."

She bit her lip and looked away from him.

"What do you want to talk to me about, Mr. Desailley? Was it the work you left me? I . . . I've finished it, though I'm afraid I didn't make a very good job of it. It was rather . . . confusing . . . and you weren't there to help me sort it out."

"For God's sake," he exclaimed roughly. "Do you really think I want to talk to you about that kind of thing after what happened tonight, Aidan?"

Her cheeks reddened slowly and her breathing quickened. Somehow she hadn't expected him to refer to what had happened on the dance floor. In a curious way, she'd relegated it to the world of fantasy, as though it had happened only in her own imagination.

Now she didn't know what to say and she looked at him quickly and then, because those inky blue eyes did such terrible things to her, she lowered her lashes.

He suddenly dropped down into a chair opposite her, stretching out his long legs and staring at her moodily from under his brows.

"You have a bad effect on me, Aidan. You know that?"

"What . . . what do you mean?" she asked huskily. All her resolutions were rapidly vanishing simply because he was there talking to her, looking at her, and she found him irresistible.

"I've told you my views on love and marriage. You're an intelligent girl and you must have realised that I have no intention in the world of forming a permanent union with any woman. Add to that the fact that you're engaged to be married, that you've obviously worked out what *you* want from life . . ."

He paused and ran his fingers distractedly through his hair, and she opened her mouth to tell him she wasn't engaged to be married, that Robert . . .

But when he went on bleakly, "I went away to think this thing through, Aidan. When I came back tonight I'd made up my mind to tell you that I don't want you around. Do you understand? *I don't want you around.* I can't work with you. You'll have to pack up your things and go."

Oh, God! Even though she'd been expecting to hear him say that for days, even though he'd as good as said it that day when he talked to Michael Hamilton on the telephone, even though she'd made up her own mind to go, she felt such shock that it seemed as though it must kill her. As though a bullet had gone straight through her heart. She felt like collapsing, and she leaned back in her chair feeling the pulse beating madly at her temples and the blood draining from her face. He didn't want her around. But what had she been expecting? A thousand miracles, of course. That was what love did to you. But when it came to love, maybe it took two to work a miracle.

She said with a strange, frozen calm, "I'm going. I've already packed, Mr. Desailley. I . . . I don't want to stay here either. I haven't found working for you exactly . . . idyllic. I'm going to Brisbane to look for work." She hadn't meant to say that, but it was out, and she stared at him almost defiantly.

"To Brisbane?" His eyebrows shot up. "And what about your fiancé? Or doesn't he matter to you? It certainly wouldn't appear so, the way your infidelities are mounting up."

Her cheeks blazed. "What do you mean, my infidelities? You're very quick to pass judgment, aren't you, Mr. Desailley?"

"Mr. Desailley," he repeated mockingly when she stopped. "It amazes me you can still call me that when we've all but gone to bed together."

"Have we? I don't remember it, Mr. . . ."

"Then you have a very short memory. Or do you think I've been unaware of your reaction to me?" He was on his feet and pacing the room restlessly. "You're typical of the women of today," he ground out. "You look for a good time wherever you can find it. Don't pretend I couldn't have got you to bed if I'd chosen to. Or that you haven't been playing around with all and sundry at the resort while I've been away."

Aidan gasped a protest but he took no notice. She could only conclude that Vanda had been telling exaggerated tales while they were dancing.

"Off to the reef all day, dining and dancing tonight . . ."

"So what did you expect me to do?" she interjected. "Stay here like a faithful hound waiting for my master to come back? I don't owe any loyalty of that kind to you, Mr. Desailley. I'm not your wife and you're not my fiancé."

"Thank heaven for that," he said. "You're a beautiful girl and I find you too damned attractive for my peace of mind, but you're like a dozen other women I know. You don't know what love is. If you did, then you'd at least show some loyalty to the man you're going to marry."

"Thank you for the lesson in morals," she exclaimed nettled. "I'd never have guessed you were qualified to set yourself up as an example from my experience of you. But if you want to know the truth, I'm not going to marry anyone. I'm not engaged to Robert."

He stopped pacing about and stared down at her. "What do you mean? When did you break it off? And why?"

"Not because of anything that's happened here," she said quickly. "It . . . it happened before I came here to work for you."

"Then why on earth did you tell me you were engaged?"

She bit her lip. Why had she told him that? It all seemed so long ago. But as far as she remembered, she'd produced Robert so Guy wouldn't think she had designs on him. Not that it had worked any too well.

"To protect myself, I suppose," she said, her voice scarcely audible. "You had enough against me without suspecting I was looking for a love affair."

He smiled crookedly. "But you were, weren't you? And you seem to have found several—though none satisfies you. And now you're leaving."

"Well, it's what you want, isn't it?" she said not looking at him.

"No. I wouldn't say it's what I *want*." There was a brief silence and then he said explosively, "Good

158

God—don't you know I think of you every hour of every day? That I have only to see you to want to take you in my arms—to kiss you to death?" He reached down suddenly and took her by the wrists, pulling her to her feet, imprisoning her against his body. She could feel his desire, and a sexual response shot through her with startling rapidity. With a muffled cry, she flung her arms around him.

"Oh, Guy, I thought you were never coming back. Where have you been?"

He hadn't attempted to kiss her and she laid her head against his chest, listening to the thudding of his heart, feeling the muscles of his back through the black shirt and holding on to him as if she would never let him go. Doing all the things she'd sworn to herself she'd never do again, in fact.

"I've been camping on a little uninhabited island," he muttered against her hair. "Thinking about you and trying to make up my mind to send you away—to carry on with my life the way I planned it. Falling in love is bad news for me. I've been fighting it every inch of the way. Not only because I thought you belonged to another man, but because it's inviting disaster."

He let her go abruptly and crossed the room to stare out across the verandah at the sea, glimmering through the palms. Aidan stood looking at him, her arms wrapped around herself, shivering in spite of the heat and the humidity. Why was it inviting disaster? Was it because his first marriage had been such an utter failure? It wouldn't be like that if she were his wife, and she ached to tell him so. To promise that she'd make him happy, that she'd understand him, that she wouldn't be jealous of his work. But how could she tell him these things when he hadn't asked her to marry him and obviously didn't intend to?

He swung round again to face her and their eyes met and clung. Like magnets they were drawn together, were back in each other's arms, though Aidan didn't know whether only one of them had moved or if they both had.

"Are you determined that I'm going to make love to you, Aidan?" he asked thickly. "Because by heaven, it's going to happen if we keep up this kind of thing. I've been tempted too often—I'm only human and I can't resist forever. I've warned you, I'm not interested in marriage, and I came back here tonight with the firm intention of telling you to pack your things and move out. That's the best thing that could happen for both of us, and you'd better remember it because I'm apt to forget it."

She bit hard on her trembling lip, not knowing what to say. Here in his arms was where she wanted to be, and her nerve ends tingled just to have him look at her the way he was doing. She drew a line across his lips with one finger and said unsteadily, "I . . . I love you, Guy."

He gave a low laugh and his hands moved to find and cup her breasts.

"Is that an invitation, Aidan? It sounds very much like it."

"I don't know," she said uncertainly, and it was only later that she realised exactly what he meant. But just at this moment she was incapable of coherent thought, particularly since he lowered his head and began kissing her fiercely, passionately. She let herself go entirely, relaxing in his arms and returning his kisses with an abandon that was quite new to her. Everything was different now that he'd admitted to falling in love with her and even though he said marriage didn't come into his calculations, she knew deep in her heart that love would change all that.

She closed her eyes, feeling the rasp of his unshaved jaw against her delicate skin.

His kisses were becoming gentler and more seductive now, and his caresses had moved from her breast to her thigh. She more than half expected him to undress her, but when he released his hold on her it was to look at her wryly and tell her, "You see—I'm getting carried away already. What are we going to do about it?"

Her grey eyes widened and soft colour came into her cheeks. Suddenly she couldn't meet his eyes, and instead she looked at his mouth, saw it curling gently, and moved infinitesimally and unconsciously closer to him.

"I shouldn't have asked you that," he said, his hands on her upper arms keeping her steady. "It's not fair to put the onus on you. It's something we have to decide together."

"How . . . do you mean?" she asked huskily.

"Whether we make love or not. Isn't that what we're talking about?"

She bit her lip, and couldn't answer.

"We can't stand here for the next half hour kissing each other and suffering frustration. Or I know I can't. Would I be welcome if I came to your room in ten minutes?"

Her lids flew up in an alarm that she tried quickly to hide, and her heart raced. Everything was moving too fast for her. It was one thing to dream of having the man you loved make love to you, but . . .

He put a finger under her chin and tilted her face up, his eyes looking into hers with a kind of quizzical mockery.

"What's the matter? Haven't you been to bed with a man before?"

She shook her head, her throat dry, and saw him grimace.

161

"I'll look after you, I promise," he said after a moment. He ran his hands down her arms and then pressed her hips against his own and told her throatily, "I want you, Aidan—God, I want you. You're not going to make me wait, are you?"

She shook her head, her nerves tense.

"Go into your room," he said, his voice low and uneven. "I'll join you in a few minutes."

She went quickly, her limbs trembling. Padding through the house on her bare feet, she reached her room, where she switched on the wall lamp and looked across at her reflection in the heart-shaped mirror. She put her hands to her cheeks. He was going to make love to her. It was going to happen. She'd said yes. Because she loved him—and he—had he said he loved her? She pulled the gold rosette from her hair, her eyes widening. What had he said? Exactly what *had* he said? "Falling in love is bad news for me." So was falling in love the same as loving?

Slowly she pulled the red dress over her head and left it in a crumpled heap on the floor. Discarding panties and bra, she went into the bathroom. She supposed she should take a shower, or wasn't there time? But there had to be time, she discovered suddenly. She just wasn't ready. Not yet.

She stayed under the shower a long time. A very long time. She just couldn't gather the courage to get out, to rub herself dry, and go into the room where her bed was and where he was coming to join her.

The minutes went by and she continued to let the lukewarm water run over her body. Her hair was wet and she knew she'd done that deliberately because it was going to take time to dry it. She listened through the sound of the shower, expecting to hear him in her room, wondering nervously if he'd open the bathroom door—come in. There was no lock, and she'd pulled the shower curtain protectively across. As if it would take more than a split second for him to draw it aside!

What had she done? she wondered, aware of her panic. He'd told her that he was not interested in marriage. He'd told her it would be the best thing for both of them for her to leave—that she must remember, because he wouldn't. In fact, the future didn't hold any promise at all for Aidan Elliot, as far as Guy Desailley was concerned. So what was she going to do? She shivered as she remembered the feel of his hands on her breasts, on her thighs, the look in his eyes as his lips found hers. She wanted him as much as he wanted her.

But what came after tonight? Nothing. He'd told her as much, and the knowledge frightened her. She just couldn't do it. She wasn't that kind of girl.

So how was she going to tell him she'd changed her mind?

She wrapped one big, soft pink towel around her, and rubbed her dripping hair with another. He was in her room now. She heard him moving softly, but he didn't come to the bathroom door. She'd been crazy not to bring a nightgown or pyjamas in here with her. She didn't have a comb, either, and when she'd all but rubbed her head off her shoulders, she raked her fingers through her hair, moistened her lips and stared at herself in the mirror. Her pupils were enormous, making her eyes look dark, and her cheeks were pale despite the tan she'd acquired. The fact was, she was scared stiff. Not because he was going to make love to her but because she had to tell him no. He was a strong, muscular man, so she had to be very composed, very rational. She'd remind him of his warning to her.

"Okay, Aidan," she could imagine him saying, taking her hands and drawing her against his naked chest. "I promise you can leave tomorrow if you like. But tonight—tonight you're going to be mine."

She'd be lost, of course. She wouldn't be able to hold out. She looked at the window. She could climb out into the garden! Why not?

Draped in a towel, but otherwise stark naked? Brilliant idea, Aidan! And once you're out there, what do you do next? Run screaming through the garden to the resort, giving anyone who sees you the idea that Guy Desailley has been trying to rape you? Alternatively, she could go along the jetty and get into the boat. There might even be some clothes there that she could put on. A pair of jeans, a man's shirt. But what was the point? Guy would come to look for her.

It really seemed there was nothing to do but face up to him. What kind of a man did she imagine he was, anyhow? He wouldn't touch her if she refused him. She knew that with absolute certainty. She'd never fallen in love with him otherwise. So perhaps it was herself she was afraid of.

Reluctantly she moved to the door and reached for the handle. Her heart was thudding; she was thinking of him there waiting for her. And she knew—oh, heaven, she knew—that she wasn't going to tell him to go away, she wasn't going to tell him any of those sensible things she'd thought out. She was going straight into his arms and whatever happened in the future would have to take care of itself. Because how could you listen to your head when your heart was thumping so loudly you were aware of nothing else?

She opened the door.

He was there. Sitting on the side of her bed. Still wearing the black pants, the black shirt. Shock went through her. She'd fastened the pink towel around her body as firmly as she could but she was still hanging on to it like grim death. She saw the look of amusement that crossed his face as she stood a few feet away from him, her eyes wide, her body trembling, her hair hanging in disarray over her bare shoulders.

He got slowly to his feet and came across to her. She felt the hardness of his fingers on her upper arms and she heard the sound as she swallowed on a dry throat.

"Aidan—I've been thinking."

So have I, she wanted to say, but she was incapable of saying a word. Her wide grey-green eyes questioned him mutely and again she saw that wry smile curve his lips and make tiny wrinkles round the darkness of his fascinating eyes.

"I shouldn't have asked what I did of you," he said softly. "I said I didn't want to get involved with you, and I meant it. But when you and I get together, everything goes haywire." He smiled down at her wryly, almost sadly. "Marriage is not for me, so let's save each other the embarrassment of ending something by not beginning it."

For a moment she stared at him uncomprehendingly. He was telling her he didn't want to make love to her after all. She just couldn't believe it; she hadn't expected it. Somewhere deep down she was hurt, badly hurt, even though she'd already decided—or thought she'd decided—that lovemaking was out, and she was agonisingly conscious of the feeling of his fingers on her bare flesh. With a sudden violent movement, she thrust his hands from her arms.

"I don't know why you're talking about marriage, Guy Desailley," she got out at last. "I'm no more interested in that than you are, believe me. And as a matter of fact, I happen to have had second thoughts too. That's why I was so long in the shower. I . . . I hoped you'd have taken the hint and disappeared before I came out."

His eyes narrowed to glittering points, and he walked across the room to stand there, his arms folded, his back to the mirror.

"That wouldn't have been very considerate of me under the circumstances. Not after you'd shown yourself so—willing," he drawled out infuriatingly.

"Well, I'm not willing now," she flung at him, grasping at her slipping towel with trembling fingers. "So please, will you go away and leave me alone? I'd like to get to bed."

"That suits me fine," he said with cold amiability. "I'll go right away. You just hop into bed and we'll forget the whole thing. Okay?"

Aidan simply couldn't answer. Forget the whole thing! Just like that! The room seemed to spin around her as he came toward her, his eyes trailing down her towel-draped figure. She stood transfixed as he ran his hand carelessly over her damp hair as though she were a child or a small animal.

"I'm going down to take a swim," he said briefly, and was gone.

Aidan heard herself sob as she sank down on the side of the bed. He was so callous, so cool and uncaring. To drop her like that—as if none of it mattered one way or the other. And it probably didn't—to him.

She felt suddenly dead tired. Hardly knowing what she was doing, she let the towel fall to the floor and crawled under the sheet.

Sheer exhaustion made her fall asleep almost instantly, but she woke in the small hours of the morning to find her mind feverishly active. Exactly where did she stand now? Her relationship with Guy had seemed to take a startling new direction last night, and then he'd negated it all at the last moment. Out of consideration for her, or simply because he'd thought better of it?

Wretchedly, she admitted to herself that it was quite

in the cards that when she got up in the morning he'd have vanished again or would be shut up in his study, and she felt she couldn't stand any more of that. Reason told her that the best thing she could do was to stick to her decision and leave.

Daylight came and she was still awake. She could hear the parrots outside, hear the faint *hush, hush* of the sea, the trembling of the palm leaves in the dawn wind. How lovely it would be to get up now before the heat of the day and go down to the beach for a swim. With Guy. And then come back and eat mangoes and drink coffee, and look across the breakfast table into his eyes. After that, he'd start work and she'd gather flowers, tidy the house, decide on the menu for the day, do some typing for him. Of course, when they had children, he'd need to employ a secretary. Someone like Diane, who had an amiable, nonsexual relationship with him.

She turned on her side and tried to think of something else, but her mind refused to leave him alone. It wandered back determinedly to last night when she'd emerged from the bathroom and found him sitting on her bed fully dressed, waiting to tell her to forget the whole thing. Suppose instead he'd been naked? Suppose he'd come to her, slipped the towel away from her body, wound his arms about her and carried her to the bed? To this bed where she lay now, alone and confused and frustrated. She wished passionately that it had happened that way.

"Oh, go to sleep, Aidan. Do as he said and forget the whole thing," she told herself wearily. How easy it had been for him to say that! And then to go down to the sea and immerse himself in the milky water. To swim, to think of other things, to banish her from his mind. Then come back to the bungalow and sleep. Not to lie awake as she lay awake.

Rigid, she listened. Perhaps he was awake and restless too. But there was not a sound in the house. Only the birds and the gently waving palms outside. She thought of her suitcase on the bench, of her clothes folded and packed away in it. She'd leave today. She was glad she'd told him she wasn't interested in him, she told herself, and was furious to find that warm tears were spilling from her eyes onto the pillowslip.

It was no use trying to fool herself. She loved him. So surely there was some way of making him understand that if he married her, it wouldn't be a repeat of what had happened to him before. She respected his work—and she loved him. But she'd already told him that, and her cheeks burned as she remembered his reaction. "Is that an invitation?"he'd said, and laughed a little. That was all it had meant to him. So be realistic, Aidan Elliot. He's told you in plain words that he's not interested in marriage. He wants to make love to you, that's all. Not even that now—for fear you have marriage on your mind.

Her lashes still wet, she drifted into sleep.

When she woke again the room was hot, and through the window across the verandah the green of the palms was dazzlingly bright in the burning sunlight. She reached for her watch on the bedside table and discovered it was after ten o'clock. She sprang up at once and hurried across to the bathroom to take a shower and wake herself up. At the door she paused. She could hear voices.

Who was it? she wondered. A masculine voice that sounded like Guy's. She couldn't hear the other voice, so it was probably a woman. Vanda?

Suddenly she decided against having a shower. She was too curious to know who it was talking to Guy.

In the bathroom she splashed her face with cool

168

water; then she came back into her room and dressed quickly in a white sundress and sandals. At the mirror she brushed her hair and tied it at one side with a green ribbon and then applied lipstick. She would have liked coffee, but that could wait. She was going straight out to look for Guy and the visitor. The voices had gone, so they must be outside, but when she reached the door and looked along the verandah, only Guy was there, wearing white shorts and a dark-blue shirt, his tanned skin looking dramatically healthy. She caught her breath at the sight of him, and felt the colour rush to her face as he rose from his chair and their eyes met. His were penetrating and hard, and they seemed to see right through to her heart.

"Good morning," she exclaimed brightly, and strolled across to the rail to shade her eyes and look out at the dazzling sea. "I'm afraid I slept late. I'm sorry about that. Was there someone here? I thought I heard voices."

"I was talking on the telephone," he said abruptly.

"Oh, who . . ." She stopped herself just in time. It wasn't her business whom he'd been speaking to, but the thought sprang up in her mind that he'd possibly been making arrangements about leaving. For both of them? Or just for her? She swung round and looked at him.

"About my leaving, Guy. I'll fit in with what you want, of course. I mean . . . if you want me to stay and . . . er . . . do some more work for you . . ."

"I don't," he interrupted harshly, and her heart sank. "I've already told you I can't work with you around. And since your fiancé's turned up, we might as well terminate your employment here and now, so you're free to make whatever arrangements you like."

Aidan was staring at him, her face paling. "My

169

fiancé? You mean Robert? But I . . . I don't understand. I told you—our engagement was broken off."

"So you did, but he still calls himself your fiancé, and according to Vanda when she rang through just now, he can hardly wait to get you to himself. I asked her to tell him you were working and would go over to the resort the minute you were free—it seemed the tactful thing to do. So I suggest you go inside now and pack your bags and get out. Leave your stuff. I'll arrange for it to be taken over to the resort as soon as possible."

As she listened, Aidan's heart went cold. She couldn't believe Robert was claiming to be her fiancé. That must be Vanda's maliciousness—it must be. Yet Guy believed it willingly. In fact, he couldn't have told her more plainly that all he wanted was to be rid of her. And although she'd made up her mind that she was leaving—or told herself she had—it hurt badly, and she knew that deep down, in her heart of hearts, there'd been a secret hope that somehow, miraculously, everything would turn out the way she wanted it. Instead, it was to end like this.

Guy had got up from his chair and stood staring down at her, his hands on his narrow hips, his dark eyes unfathomable, and suddenly, losing control of herself, she burst out, "You're wrong about me and Robert, Guy. I told you last night it was all over between us."

A nerve jerked at his jawline. "You've told me a number of things, Aidan. First you're engaged; then you're not. As for anything you told me last night—I think we can both forget it. The fact remains that you're a marrying kind of girl and your fiancé is here now. Well, that suits me fine. I know my own nature too well to make an issue of it, and I surrender you unreservedly to his loving care. But don't ask me to meet him. And I hope you're suitably grateful that I didn't grab what you were offering me last night. It would have been very easy for me to take it."

"It wouldn't," she denied, her cheeks blazing. "I told you I'd changed my mind. When I came out from the shower and you were still there I was going to tell you no."

He smiled crookedly. "No would soon have changed to yes. I know what your resistance is like. It's very weak."

She bit her lip. Where he was concerned, that was true and she knew it.

"All right. Then I'm grateful to you—for just that one thing. But for nothing else. I shan't remember this interlude in my life with gratitude."

"How will you remember it, then?"

She shook her head, aware that tears were very close to the surface. "I'll forget it." She turned away and went inside.

Forget it? Not in a million years. Although that was exaggerating—of course she'd forget it. But probably not until she was old, really old. Or until she'd fallen in love again. Which would be never.

It was not until she reached her room and began to pack away her few remaining things that she really gave a thought to Robert. Why had he come here? In spite of what Guy believed, Aidan knew very well he didn't want to marry her. He wasn't in love with her and never had been. Now if the house had been hers . . . But it was not hers, and never would be, and she wished passionately that Robert had stayed safely in Sydney, minding his own business, instead of coming here to pester her again, for whatever reason. Then things might have been very different today.

Yet what was the use of fooling herself? Guy had never pretended even for a moment that he'd ever marry her. "Marriage is not for me," he'd told her in plain words. And the fact was, he was quite right in his assessment of her. She was a marrying kind of girl. Unfortunately.

She sighed and continued with the unhappy task of clearing the last of her belongings from the drawers.

Chapter Ten

About a half hour later, Aidan left for the resort. Guy had wished her an indifferent good-bye and barely glanced at her, which was just as well—she was ready to burst into tears. Yet somehow she'd managed to be equally casual as she said good-bye to him. He'd rung through to the resort while she was packing to arrange accommodations for her, and before she left he told her coolly, "Just how long you stay is up to you and your fiancé."

Since Aidan had already denied that Robert was her fiancé she didn't bother to do so again, and neither did she inform him that she intended to stay on the island no longer than it would take her to make arrangements to leave. With or without Robert.

As she took the path through the wild garden to the resort for the very last time, she didn't dare to dwell on her thoughts, which were all of Guy, but instead tried to make her mind a blank. But Guy was there, heartache was there, and she wanted to weep. With an immense effort, she forced herself to think of Robert. She didn't look forward to seeing him, and she couldn't think of any reason why he should have come here. Much less why he should be claiming to be her fiancé. That for sure was a lie Vanda had told, possibly in revenge for Aidan's interfering between herself and Guy. Though that was ludicrous. Vanda would never persuade Guy to marry her. Aidan didn't think anyone would ever manage to do that. He was so cynical about love and marriage.

Realising that her thoughts had returned to Guy, she began to walk more purposefully, and to go over in her mind what she had to do.

Go to Reception first of all, not only to find out where Robert was, but even more importantly to make some inquiries about leaving the island. She had yet to make up her mind whether she'd go back to Sydney or whether she'd stop off in Brisbane and look for work there. That idea didn't appeal to her very much. She had no friends in Brisbane, and she had a feeling she was going to need friends badly for the next little while.

As for Robert—his presence here was a mystery that had yet to be solved.

Louise Hardy was at Reception when Aidan walked in, and she glared at her unsmilingly.

"Yes?" she asked in icy tones.

"I'm looking for one of the guests," Aidan said, icy too, and refusing to refer to Robert as a friend. "Mr. Fuller. Could you tell me which is his lodge?"

Louise Hardy brightened slightly. "Ah, yes—Vanda told me he's expecting you. A very special friend of yours, isn't he? Well, you'll find him in unit number five, down toward the beach on your left as you leave the office."

"Thank you. Could you also tell me if it would be possible to get over to the mainland today?"

174

"Yes." The answer was prompt, even eager. "If you take the launch that leaves the jetty at two o'clock, you'll connect with another one on Wilcox Island. But don't tell me you're thinking of leaving us," Louise added with patently false regret.

"Yes, I am, Mrs. Hardy. I know Guy reserved a suite for me, but I shan't be needing it. I apologise."

"That's quite all right," the older woman cooed. "And your fiancé—will he be leaving too?"

"If you're talking about Mr. Fuller, I have no idea what his plans are," Aidan said. "And by the way, when my luggage is brought over from the bungalow, will you please hold it here for me?"

"Certainly. Better than that, I'll arrange for it to be taken down to the jetty before two o'clock."

"Thank you." Aidan left the office briskly and just outside almost ran into Vanda.

"Oh—hello, Aidan!" The other girl was all smiles. "I guess you're thrilled to bits that your boyfriend's turned up. He rang you a couple of times, but apparently decided eventually the easiest thing was to present himself in person. You're so elusive, I just never managed to get a message to you."

Aidan looked at her steadily. "How hard did you try, Vanda?"

Vanda widened her brown eyes. "Oh, I tried, Aidan. But you never answered the phone. And last night I didn't want to embarrass you by bursting in on your little twosome with the glad news that your fiancé was on his way here."

Aidan frowned. "What makes you think Mr. Fuller's my fiancé, Vanda?"

"Well, isn't he?" Vanda asked innocently. "It was the most acceptable explanation I could think of for such ardour. Well, I won't hold you up. Enjoy yourself!"

She drifted off, and Aidan walked on thoughtfully. So she had been right. Vanda had had a hand in all this. If Robert had left a message, she'd deliberately not passed it on.

As she drew near the lodge, set in among the palms that fringed the beach, she saw Robert come onto the porch and pause to put on his sunglasses. He was very presentable, very good-looking, in fact, and just now he was immaculate in a light-blue denim jacket and matching pants. But her heart didn't jump at the sight of him. In fact it stayed so quiet, she might not have had a heart at all. She thought uneasily of her immediate and wild physical response to Guy, and wondered if she was deluding herself in believing that he reacted to her in something of the same way. The big difference, of course, was that his heart was not involved, whereas hers was.

Robert had seen her by now and came quickly to meet her. He hardly looked the ardent lover, Aidan thought. His stride was purposeful, and his smile businesslike rather than anything else.

"At last!" he greeted her. "I suppose I've interrupted your work, Aidan, but I don't have a lot of time, and I have to see you. Come and sit down while we talk."

A little mystified, Aidan agreed, and as they settled down on the cane chairs in the shade of the porch, she asked him bluntly, "What's this all about, Robert? You are interrupting me, you know. Couldn't you have written, or rung?"

He took his sunglasses off and stared at her, his expression changing to one of annoyance.

"Rung? What else do you think I've been doing the last few days except ring you? Why do you think I'm here now?"

Aidan grimaced. "I'm afraid I haven't the slightest

176

idea. And if you're taking me to task for not ringing you," she added hotly, "I didn't even know you wanted me to. Apparently Vanda found it too difficult to contact me. So if you want to blame anyone, blame her."

"Oh." He looked slightly taken aback. "Well, let's forget it. Shay told me you weren't coming back to Sydney but meant to go to Brisbane, and I didn't want you to disappear before I had a chance to talk to you. About your aunt's house, of course. That's why I'm here."

Of course! Aidan gritted her teeth. Robert was impossible. He seemed incapable of getting it into his head that she wasn't going to contest the will.

"You know what I feel about my aunt's house, Robert," she said exasperatedly. "As far as I'm concerned there's nothing to talk about. Why can't you accept that, for goodness' sake, and leave me alone?"

"Because I happen to want that house badly," he said stubbornly. "For almost a year I've dreamed of turning it into a showplace. It would make my reputation as an architect. Don't you realise that? It would also be worth a fortune by the time I'd made my dream a reality."

"Well, I'm sorry, Robert," Aidan said shortly. "You're wasting your time talking to me about it. There's nothing I can do. Unless you can come up with enough money to buy it."

Robert put on his sunglasses again. "There is something," he said then. "Otherwise I wouldn't be here. Listen—I've been talking to Michael Hamilton, and he tells me that you and he are jointly responsible for the sale of the property. Well, the market's tight, and you're not going to shift a house like that easily. Michael's already discovering that. So what I suggest is that you persuade him to agree on the price my father's prepared to put up. He will—particularly if you and I are going to be married. And that's the other thing I wanted to discuss with you before you disappeared to Brisbane or wherever." He paused and smiled at her, and though she thought he looked very handsome, she could hardly keep her contempt from showing in her face. "How about it, Aidan?"

"I don't think so," she said coolly. "My aunt left her house to benefit a charitable organisation, and I wouldn't dream of asking Michael to accept less than a fair price for it. Nor would I dream of marrying you," she finished, rather more vehemently than she'd intended. She stood up quickly, and when he would have spoken, she told him abruptly, "There's really nothing more to say. And now if you'll excuse me, I want to see about my luggage. I'm leaving here today."

Without even saying good-bye, she turned her back on him and hurried away, wondering irritably how she'd ever thought herself in love with a man as mercenary as that.

She didn't have to see about her luggage, of course, and she had no idea of what she was going to do. All she'd wanted was to get away from Robert. But somehow her footsteps led her of their own accord in the direction of the white gate, and she went through it and hurried along the path. She just had to see Guy once more before she left. Perhaps when he knew she'd told him the truth about Robert, he'd allow her to stay—just until he left the island himself. She didn't really think it would happen, but she had to try.

But when she reached the bungalow it was to find it empty and silent. She looked into all the rooms and then went through the verandah to the beach. The boats had gone.

She couldn't believe it. She was too late, and it was all she could do not to burst into tears. Now there was nothing for it but to go. Her luggage had vanished, so presumably it had been taken over to the resort. It was lunchtime, but she wasn't hungry, and she couldn't bear the thought of running into Robert again. With a curious feeling of unreality, she made herself some tea in the kitchen, and then washed the few dishes that were still in the kitchen. Before two o'clock she was on the jetty, dry-eyed and unhappy.

She went to Brisbane and stayed there a week, and in her small hotel room, she felt lonelier than she'd ever felt in her life. She didn't find any work, but that was partly because she didn't have the heart or the energy to look for it. Guy haunted her thoughts, waking or sleeping, and finally she decided to go back to Sydney. Before, she'd been afraid of the idea of encountering him at the Hamiltons'; now she longed for it. She didn't care if he hated her, if he ignored her, just so long as she could see him and know that he still existed.

Shay was delighted to see her, reproached her for not letting her know she was coming and then said she was glad she'd decided against Brisbane after all. In fact, to Aidan's surprise, she appeared to think she'd come straight down from Breakaway Island. Which meant, Aidan realised with a feeling of bitter disappointment, that Guy couldn't have come to Sydney. So where was he? she wondered desperately.

"Where's Robert?" Shay wanted to know. "I've been longing to know what happened up there on the island. He seemed determined to persuade you to get engaged to him again. I didn't think you'd want him around, and I must admit I tried to stop him from taking off. But he got into such a panic when I said you meant to find work in Brisbane that I came to the conclusion he must be really keen."

Aidan managed a smile. "I don't think he was all that keen. And to tell you the truth I don't know where he is and I don't care. So you can see I'm definitely not going to marry him."

"Hmm," Shay said thoughtfully. She'd followed Aidan into the bedroom and sat watching her as she began to unpack a few of her things. "What did you mean when you said you didn't get on with Guy?"

Aidan braced herself. She'd known she'd have to face questions, and she knew she couldn't tell Shay or anyone the truth. She concentrated on hanging some clothes in the wardrobe and kept her face turned away as she said lightly, "Well, as you know—I wasn't the sort of secretary he wanted at all. So it just didn't work out," she finished lamely.

"I'm sorry about that," Shay said after a moment. "I had a silly sort of idea that you two might hit it off. Not just on a working basis but . . . personally. Michael was ropeable when I told him what I'd done. He said Guy liked someone mature and sensible and business-like, that you'd be a disturbing influence."

"He was right," Aidan said. "That's exactly what I was. Now tell me what's been happening here while I've been away. Has anyone shown any interest in buying Aunt's house?"

"Well, Robert's father put out a feeler," Shay said cautiously. "Mike had the idea that you and Robert must be planning to marry after all and that you'd suggested to Robert that—well, that he might make a deal about purchasing the property. We've heard no more about it, but anyway, Mike was going to wait till you came back to discuss it with you."

"There's nothing to discuss," Aidan said, feeling angry with Robert. "As far as I'm concerned, we'll get as good a price as we can for that house. I have no desire to cheat all those poor little kids out of the help Aunt Sylvia wanted to give them.''

"I must admit it didn't sound like one of your ideas,'' Shay said. "So with Robert still out of the picture, I suppose you're going to look for work again. When's Guy coming down to Sydney, by the way?''

"I haven't the least idea,'' Aidan said, and Shay laughed.

"You really sound as if you'd had enough of him, Aidan. It must have been mere wishful thinking on my part to imagine you two would hit it off. As a match-maker, I seem to be a complete failure.''

"Just don't try again,'' Aidan warned, keeping her voice deliberately light. "I'm not interested in marriage at the moment.''

"Pity,'' Shay said. "It's something I'd definitely recommend. Though of course you have to team up with the right man.''

"Exactly,'' Aidan agreed, and hoped Shay didn't hear the bitter note in her voice.

Two weeks went by. The house wasn't sold—finances were tight, Michael said—and Aidan didn't find work. She decided to advertise that she'd type manuscripts or documents or anything at all at home, and she began looking for a small flat for herself. She couldn't expect to live with the Hamiltons forever.

She heard nothing of Robert, and for that she was thankful. Guy's name came up every now and again in conversation at the dinner table, and each time Aidan felt her pulses race. But Michael heard nothing from him, so presumably he wasn't in Sydney. Aidan had the feeling of being under constant tension, and she real-ised that the sooner she moved out of the Hamiltons' house, the better it would be for her. As long as she was here, she couldn't keep Guy out of her mind, and each day she dreaded yet hoped Michael would have news that he was in Sydney.

Then quite suddenly, it happened.

She'd actually arranged to move out and take a room in a terrace house near the University of Sydney, where she should get plenty of home typing if she couldn't find herself a regular job, when Michael rang through from work and asked to speak to her.

"Aidan—great news! It looks like we have a buyer at last."

"Marvellous!" she enthused. "Someone with the money?"

"Definitely. And perfectly happy to pay our price," Michael said. "And now I want to ask a favour of you, Aidan, though I'm afraid you mightn't be any too pleased. I had hoped to be at the house myself this afternoon, but now I find I can't get away. I was wondering if you'd go along and take over for me."

"Of course I'll go," she said at once. "Though I'll admit it might make me feel a bit weepy, if that's what you're worried about."

"Well, no, it's not exactly that," he admitted and then went on carefully. "The buyer happens to be Guy Desailley and I know you two didn't get on too well together."

Guy Desailley! Aidan leaned back in the chair, feeling as if she could scarcely breathe. "It's all right," she said faintly. "Did he . . . ask after me?"

"Not exactly. He wanted to know if your house was still on the market, that's all. But we didn't have a long conversation, and we hadn't got around to personalities. I'm sure he'll be very pleasant to you, so don't worry. But if you really feel you'd rather not handle it, I'll ask Shay."

"Oh, no," Aidan said quickly. "I'll go, if you'll just tell me what time to expect him."

"Great! Be there about three," Michael told her. He added a few words of advice that she scarcely heard, and when she hung up she found Shay had come into the room and was looking at her anxiously.

"What's the matter? You're as white as a ghost. What's Michael been telling you?"

"Nothing," she said shakily. "He wants me to go over to the house this afternoon to show it to a prospective buyer. Guy Desailley."

"Guy!" Shay's eyes lit up for a moment, and then she frowned. "Does it make you feel that bad? The thought of selling the house?"

Aidan shook her head. She felt utterly confused. She simply couldn't answer and Shay came and sat on the arm of the chair.

"Aidan—what is it? Do you really hate Guy that much? Or did you fall in love with him?"

Aidan nodded miserably. It was a relief to admit it. "But he wasn't interested." She found a tissue and blew her nose. "Don't worry, I'm just about over it."

She didn't know if Shay believed her or not.

She was in the house well before three o'clock, and despite the trauma of meeting Guy again she was filled with an intense feeling of nostalgia.

She stood at the huge windows of the sitting room looking out at the brilliant blue of the Pacific Ocean. Far down below was the beach, the sunbathers scattered along its golden curve looking tiny from this height. Guy would love it, she knew instinctively, and she couldn't help imagining how wonderful it would be to live here with him—to plan the renovations and redecorating together. Why she allowed such crazy thoughts to come into her mind she didn't know. She should have let Shay come, of course. Seeing him again was only going to make it worse for herself afterward.

183

She sank down into one of the comfortable old black leather armchairs, and staring out at the sparkling ocean she thought of a lot of things. Of Sylvia and all the years they'd lived here together; of that all too brief last year when they both knew Sylvia's life was nearing its end; of her engagement to Robert, which now seemed totally unreal but which had made her aunt happy, because she believed Aidan would have someone to love and cherish her. Yet all the time Robert had been thinking only of possessing this house.

Her thoughts were interrupted by the ringing of the doorbell and she jumped to her feet in a panic. Guy! He was early! And oh—her hair needed tidying, and she had sudden doubts as to how she looked in her trim green pants and green silk shirt. She discovered she'd been crying, and she wiped her eyes hastily on the back of her hand as she hurried up the shallow steps that led from the big sitting room into the entrance hall that was a room in itself.

She'd left the door open, and silhouetted against the daylight was Guy's tall, broad-shouldered figure. Her heart began to race and she wanted to run to him and throw herself into his arms.

Instead, she halted a few paces from him and greeted him almost formally, hoping he didn't notice the tremor in her voice.

"Hello, Mr. Desailley. I'm sorry Michael couldn't get here this afternoon to show you the house. I'm afraid you'll have to put up with me. Will you please come in? The great thing is the view, of course, so I'll show you that first."

She led the way back through the hall into the sitting room, where everyone, when he first came here, was simply struck dumb. She turned to look at Guy, expecting to see that rapt look on his face. Instead, she found she was staring straight into his eyes. Dark midnight blue and turning her bones to water. With a little gasp of shock, she moved across to the windows and stood there with her back to him.

"That's Whale Beach down there. It's a long, steep walk, but of course by car it's nothing. It's a topless beach . . ."

She broke off trembling as his hands gripped her arms and he said savagely, "For heavens' sake, Aidan —stop babbling inanities as if I were a stranger and you were trying to sell me something."

"But I . . . I am," she said huskily, too conscious of the warmth of his fingers through the silk of her blouse, feeling again that almost irresistible impulse to turn to him—to raise her lips to his.

"You're hating it, aren't you?" he said, his thumbs probing her flesh. "You must be wishing there were some way you could hang on to the property—live here when you marry. Can't that fiancé of yours raise the cash to buy the place? I thought you said he had money."

Aidan flinched and pulled away from him. "That fiancé" of hers was cropping up again and it was just too much to bear.

"You don't seem able to understand that I don't have a fiancé, Mr. Desailley," she said swinging round to face him. She saw his dark brow rise and then straighten.

"Exactly what's that supposed to mean, *Miss Elliot?* he asked mockingly. "I've been given to understand you spent several days on Breakaway Island with your—with Robert. That you left the island together. So what's happened this time? Another temporary break while you enjoy yourself with someone else?"

"Nothing of the kind," she said tautly. "I didn't spend several days with Robert, and I can't think what gave you the idea that I did—particularly since you left the island even before I did."

"Just what are you trying to say?" he asked after a moment. "When I came back to Breakaway, I picked up what happened from a few remarks Vanda made."

Aidan looked at him angrily. Vanda seemed to have been putting her finger in every pie in sight, and even though it would probably do no good at all, she was going to tell Guy a few plain facts. "You may not believe me," she told him, her head up, her eyes flashing, "but I left the island the day Robert arrived. I have no idea what he did. I haven't seen him since, and I don't want to see him. He came to talk business, that's all. It's this house he loves, not me," she finished flatly.

He was looking at her narrowly, and suddenly her eyes were trapped by his inky blue gaze, and everything changed. Her anger vanished as her glance moved slowly over him, taking in the thick, curling black hair; the tanned skin; the firm jawline, freshly shaven; the mouth with its slightly sensual lower lip that had a quizzical upward quirk at one corner, so that she longed to trace its line with a finger.

She heard him draw a deep breath; then he reached out and pulled her into his arms. She went unresistingly, and then they were kissing—passionately, dementedly, as if they must kiss or die. Aidan clung to him, her body moulding itself to his as his mouth explored hers.

When he took his mouth from hers it was to draw her down with him onto the black leather couch, his arms still holding her tightly. Aidan closed her eyes and relaxed against him. This was a dream, of course; it had nothing to do with reality. With a feeling of dread she recalled other times when he'd held her to him like this and made love to her—only to push her from him, to tell her he didn't want her around.

"Let's go back to the beginning," he said after a long moment. "You're not going to marry Robert?"

She shook her head.

"Why not?"

"Because I don't love him." Her voice was no more than a murmur. With an effort she drew away from him and sat up, pushing her hair back, looking out at the dazzling sea that was all that could be seen from the window. "Hadn't we better get on with . . . with what you're here for? Michael said I must show you the house."

"I don't give a damn about the house," he said violently. "Have you been telling me the truth, Aidan? You're not going to marry Robert?"

"I'm not going to marry anybody." She could feel her cheeks flush a hectic red; but when she tried to get up from the couch he held her back and swept her into his arms again. And then he was saying—though she was still sure she must be dreaming, because he couldn't possibly have said that—"Marry me, Aidan."

She struggled away from him. "Marry you? You . . . you're not interested in marriage. I don't want to ruin your life."

"You've ruined it already," he groaned. "I can't live without you. Oh, God, I know what you must think of me—I've told you in many ways that I don't trust women, that I can't work with you around. But the fact is I can't work without you. I know that now. I've learned it the hard way. Nothing's worthwhile if you aren't there. I've never felt this way in my life before, Aidan, and it's agony."

They were kissing again and Aidan's whole world was spinning so that she felt dizzy. This just couldn't be true—and yet she knew that it was, that it had to be. It was meant to be. It was why she had gone to Breakaway Island—to meet Guy, to discover the pain of love, and now, to discover its joy. She heard him whispering against her hair, "Marry me, Aidan—say you'll marry me."

"Oh, Guy," she whispered back. "Yes—yes—of course I will."

Their lips met and clung again and she felt herself in seventh heaven.

"I never thought this would happen to me," he murmured when they drew apart. "I never thought I'd want a woman in my life again. Be very sure what you're going into, my darling—I'm not an easy man to live with; I'm obsessed by my work. Though God knows, I'm inclined to think from now on my wants, my desires, are going to be very different."

"I'll be happy anyway," she murmured. "So long as you love me. I know what your work means to you. I'll be content to have what's left over."

"It'll be a pretty big percentage," he said smiling down into her eyes. "I won't dare to leave you alone— I'll be too jealous."

"Don't say that," she begged. "As if I weren't to be trusted. I love you too much ever to want anyone else."

They were in each other's arms once more, but before he kissed her again there was something that she had to know.

"Guy, Vanda said you were in love with her . . ."

He shook his head. "Never. We had a love affair of sorts before I went overseas. Nothing serious—never any talk of marriage. You're the only woman I want to share my life with. Kiss me—promise me . . ."

She looked deep into his eyes and asked him seriously, "Do you trust me, Guy?"

"With my life," he murmured, and with a sigh of contentment she abandoned herself to him.

Silhouette **Romance**

15-Day Free Trial Offer
6 Silhouette Romances

6 Silhouette Romances, free for 15 days! We'll send you 6 new Silhouette Romances to keep for 15 days, absolutely free! If you decide not to keep them, send them back to us. You pay nothing.

Free Home Delivery. But if you enjoy them as much as we think you will, keep them by paying the invoice enclosed with your free trial shipment. We'll pay all shipping and handling charges. You get the convenience of Home Delivery and we pay the postage and handling charge each month.

Don't miss a copy. The Silhouette Book Club is the way to make sure you'll be able to receive every new romance we publish before they're sold out. There is no minimum number of books to buy and you can cancel at any time.

This offer expires October 31, 1983

Silhouette Book Club, Dept. SBZ 17B
120 Brighton Road, Clifton, NJ 07012

   Please send me 6 Silhouette Romances to keep for 15 days, absolutely free. I understand I am not obligated to join the Silhouette Book Club unless I decide to keep them.

NAME_____

ADDRESS_____

CITY_____STATE_____ZIP_____

Silhouette Romance

IT'S YOUR OWN SPECIAL TIME
Contemporary romances for today's women.
Each month, six very special love stories will be yours
from SILHOUETTE. Look for them wherever books are sold
or order now from the coupon below.

$1.50 each

☐ 5 Goforth	☐ 28 Hampson	☐ 54 Beckman	☐ 83 Halston
☐ 6 Stanford	☐ 29 Wildman	☐ 55 LaDame	☐ 84 Vitek
☐ 7 Lewis	☐ 30 Dixon	☐ 56 Trent	☐ 85 John
☐ 8 Beckman	☐ 32 Michaels	☐ 57 John	☐ 86 Adams
☐ 9 Wilson	☐ 33 Vitek	☐ 58 Stanford	☐ 87 Michaels
☐ 10 Caine	☐ 34 John	☐ 59 Vernon	☐ 88 Stanford
☐ 11 Vernon	☐ 35 Stanford	☐ 60 Hill	☐ 89 James
☐ 17 John	☐ 38 Browning	☐ 61 Michaels	☐ 90 Major
☐ 19 Thornton	☐ 39 Sinclair	☐ 62 Halston	☐ 92 McKay
☐ 20 Fulford	☐ 46 Stanford	☐ 63 Brent	☐ 93 Browning
☐ 22 Stephens	☐ 47 Vitek	☐ 71 Ripy	☐ 94 Hampson
☐ 23 Edwards	☐ 48 Wildman	☐ 73 Browning	☐ 95 Wisdom
☐ 24 Healy	☐ 49 Wisdom	☐ 76 Hardy	☐ 96 Beckman
☐ 25 Stanford	☐ 50 Scott	☐ 78 Oliver	☐ 97 Clay
☐ 26 Hastings	☐ 52 Hampson	☐ 81 Roberts	☐ 98 St. George
☐ 27 Hampson	☐ 53 Browning	☐ 82 Dailey	☐ 99 Camp

$1.75 each

☐ 100 Stanford	☐ 110 Trent	☐ 120 Carroll	☐ 130 Hardy
☐ 101 Hardy	☐ 111 South	☐ 121 Langan	☐ 131 Stanford
☐ 102 Hastings	☐ 112 Stanford	☐ 122 Scofield	☐ 132 Wisdom
☐ 103 Cork	☐ 113 Browning	☐ 123 Sinclair	☐ 133 Rowe
☐ 104 Vitek	☐ 114 Michaels	☐ 124 Beckman	☐ 134 Charles
☐ 105 Eden	☐ 115 John	☐ 125 Bright	☐ 135 Logan
☐ 106 Dailey	☐ 116 Lindley	☐ 126 St. George	☐ 136 Hampson
☐ 107 Bright	☐ 117 Scott	☐ 127 Roberts	☐ 137 Hunter
☐ 108 Hampson	☐ 118 Dailey	☐ 128 Hampson	☐ 138 Wilson
☐ 109 Vernon	☐ 119 Hampson	☐ 129 Converse	☐ 139 Vitek

Silhouette Romance

Coming next month from
Silhouette Romances

The Dawn Is Golden by Anne Hampson

Melanie believed her only means of escape was to flee with Vidas Loudaros to his Greek island. Once there she found herself faced with trading her innocence for freedom!

Practical Dreamer by Dixie Browning

Thane Coulter shattered Tally's poised professional front whenever he came near, and yet, he was the only man who could pick up all the pieces.

Two Faces Of Love by Mary Carroll

Marcello's insistent love-making had dazzled Gina, but his enigmatic behavior was breaking her heart. Gina realized too late that she was in love with a man who didn't need her.

A Private Eden by Ashley Summers

Upset that Gabe had deceived her, Sara no longer knew what to think about the man she found so seductively attractive . . . but who continued to elude her love.

Hidden Isle by Ruth Langan

Morgan was capable, sincere, and in love with screenwriter Kent Taylor. Alone with him on his Canadian island retreat, she longed to show Kent her love—before he left the island and her life forever.

Delta River Magic by Edith St. George

Powerless to say no to Chase Barrister, her handsome, enigmatic boss, Francine accompanied his godmother on a cruise down the Mississippi. Only Francine didn't realize she'd be accompanying Chase as well!